Let the Ghosts Sleep

Keller Agre

UNDERTAKER BOOKS

Cover Artist: Roderick Brydon

First edition 2025

Contents

Praise for "Let the Ghosts Sleep"

"Agre takes debut horror to a whole new level with an ominously addictive ghost tale that will leave you second guessing your next vacation—for better or worse." – Laura Bilodeau, author of *Dr. Grinsaw*

"A classic ghost story in the vein of Matheson, Poe, or Jackson---filled with mystery---color me impressed. I'll be watching for more from this author and you should too" – Chisto Healy, best-selling author of *The Gateway in Apartment 8*

"Fast-paced, scary, fun, dark, a little whiskey, all the things that make a solid story. The ghosts may sleep; you will not." – Michael Carter, author of *Boneyard Tales*

"Let the Ghosts Sleep is a classic ghost story filtered through a darker, more modern lens. Agre paints a vivid picture of a haunted hotel off the coast of Georgia. The secrets of Crane Island will stay with you for a long time." – Bryan Holm, Author of *Satanic Static*

"Keller Agre's debut novella Let the Ghosts Sleep is an examination of fame culture, the occasional exploitative nature of true crime podcasts, and the lengths one will go to stay relevant and rich. Featuring an unlikable main character I loved to hate and the literal and metaphorical ghosts of his past, Agre provides a refreshing, twisty take on classic haunting tropes, culminating in a satisfying, full-circle conclusion. You won't wanna "sleep" on this one!" – Chloe York, author of *Our Devil's Awake*

"Let the Ghosts Sleep carries a wisp of old-fashioned southern charm, not unlike the Georgia coast it visits. As an ambitious podcast host examines two serial killers more than a hundred years apart, the ghosts — both literal and figurative — in this novella scratch at the thin veneer of Deep South gentility, money, and fame addiction, exposing the ugliness beneath them. A haunting read from a new voice in horror." – Michael Wehunt, author of *The October Film Haunt* and *Greener Pastures*

To my partner, Caitlin.

LET THE GHOSTS SLEEP

FRIDAY, JUNE 7, 2024

"...AND THAT'S OUR SHOW. Will the Marie College Maimer strike again this weekend?

"As a reminder, The Cadaver Hour, *America's favorite true crime podcast, will be back next week. I need to escape the merciless grasp the Maimer has on our city! Who knows? I could be his next victim.*

"To avoid that, your beloved host will be traveling this weekend on a special assignment. I'll be staying at the Crane Island Club Resort on the Georgia coast to report on the infamous murders that occurred there in the spring of 1901. Maybe I'll even find out who the Crane Island Killer was! Will I encounter one of the ghosts that supposedly haunt the resort's halls? Will I meet a grisly end like those unfortunate souls who stayed there over a hundred years ago? If you don't hear from me next week, send help!

"Thanks for listening. And as always, don't let yourself become the subject of my next episode."

I took the headphones off and let my sound engineer, Kurt, get the show ready for upload. I didn't bother with post-production tasks since my show became the most listened-to true crime podcast in the country, and I was able to hire him. It wasn't popular due to my unmatched research skills or Kurt's editing. Hank Blight, my podcast name, had a voice and presence people craved. I spent less and less time talking about the cases as the years passed. My personality was enough to keep listeners engaged. That and the Maimer.

"Do you think he's going to kill again this weekend?" Kurt asked, working away on his laptop.

"I sure hope so. Ratings have been amazing this month."

"You hope so?" Kurt asked, grimacing. "What about the families?"

"Haven't you been listening? The families are never around much, are they? Whoever he is, he's not exactly striking down pillars of the community."

"But that one, Helen Grier. She had kids. And all those college students..."

"And what about Brian Stevens? Do you remember him?"

"You know I do," Kurt said. "But that was different."

"Look, Kurt, we can't get too invested. We'd go crazy if we put ourselves in each pair of bloody shoes. People die every day."

"I guess," Kurt said.

"You go to a different college anyway. You didn't know any of them."

"You're right."

I wasn't convinced any of my words made it through.

"Any plans this weekend, buddy?" I asked.

"Not really, Mr. Hall. I'll probably go to the grocery store, maybe watch a few movies. I have my sister's graduation on Sunday."

"Please, call me 'Henry.' We've talked about this."

"Sorry."

"It's fine. You have to get out of your apartment. Meet a girl. Go to the bar. Just sit there and read. Girls love stuff like that."

"You know I don't drink."

"...Right. Well...you don't need to order drinks. Get one of those...mocktails."

"All right," Kurt said, keeping his eyes on the screen.

I headed toward the studio's exit.

"Are you nervous at all?" Kurt asked, catching me before I could leave.

"About what?"

"You know...the ghosts."

"You don't believe that crap, do you?"

"No," Kurt said, breaking eye contact.

"I'm just going for a much-needed relaxing weekend. We've both been working too much."

Kurt laughed to himself a little too hard and said, "True."

"I'll make up a few ghost stories. Take a shaky video for the website. Maybe I'll even hire someone to stand in a dark corner. You'll have the notes by Monday."

"Sounds good," Kurt said, shutting his laptop.

"I want to hear about your weekend when I get back," I said, unsure if Kurt was even listening. "I don't want to find out on Monday the most exciting thing you did was watch another Japanese horror flick."

"Sure thing." Kurt flashed a weak smile. "Have a good weekend."

I gave a two-finger wave and was outside. The sun reflected off my new EV, making me squint. I hopped inside, cranked up my favorite music, and rolled the windows down, dosing the neighborhood with the greatest pop-punk hits.

About halfway home, at a red light, I saw a man on the corner, holding a "Give me money" sign. He started dancing to my music. Would the Maimer target him? How many listeners would tune in if another killing happened over the weekend? The Maimer nearly doubled our average listeners each time he collected another victim.

A car horn beeped behind me, letting me know the light had turned green. I flicked the honker the bird and stepped on the gas. Well, the electricity.

After a few more traffic lights, I parked inside my condo's garage, plugged my car in, and headed inside. My suitcase lay open on my bed, partially packed. I topped it off with clothes, my favorite cologne, and a book I probably wouldn't read.

Rambo, my three-year-old husky, joined me to "help." He always seemed to know when I was about to leave him. He hovered at my feet, yelping for attention. I tripped over him on more than one occasion until I was forced to shut him in one of the other rooms so I could breathe. Maybe a smaller dog would've been a better choice. I had almost no yard to speak of and the Atlanta summers were tough on him. Not to mention the thing shed like crazy. But I liked how he looked. Plus, women love big dogs.

I zipped up my suitcase and threw it in my car. I practically carried Rambo to the passenger's seat. He knew where we were going, and he didn't like it. In a few minutes, we were at the doggy daycare. The smell of piss and hair made me cover my nose when I first walked in.

"Mr. Hall?" the woman asked.

"Yes. And y'all know Rambo."

"We do," she said with a polite smile. "Just a reminder, he only has one more strike before we'll have to ask you to find another daycare."

"Thanks," I said.

I handed over the leash and left before any stink could seep into my clothes.

The drive would be four hours, a distance I hadn't driven for a while. Now that I had the money, I always opted for a flight when one was available. To pass the time, I put on my favorite true crime podcast, other than my own, of course, and turned my brain off. Their production quality was higher, but the co-host got on my nerves. I will admit, balancing the facts while maintaining some personality was a tough job and one they needed more than one person to accomplish.

I passed the unexciting central Georgia landscape, full of pine trees and "heritage" sites. How could people live in some of these towns? Some of us had a harder start to life, but couldn't they just move? Not everyone was as lucky as me, unburdened by family responsibilities. I felt bad for those who were constrained by circumstances they couldn't control.

The monotonous drive reminded me of why I started taking planes. Although, some of the rural billboards kept me entertained. As always on long car rides, even as a kid, I found myself thinking about things I had no control over. Things I wished I could do better and things I promised myself I'd do, or wouldn't do, in the future.

Excerpt from The Cadaver Hour (originally recorded October 1, 2023)

"...Next on our show, a new killer has emerged on the Atlanta streets. Make sure your kids are home safe because according to police, two murders occurred over the weekend, both on Marie College's campus. Two bodies were found floating in the campus pond. The same pond your podcast host frequents. In fact, If I had taken my morning walk a few hours earlier, I could've been the one who found them. If I had found them, I would've been horrified with what I saw. And smelled.

"The victims were a pair of 19-year-old undergrads. The man and woman were strangled after leaving the library late Friday night. Had they heard of parties? Maybe they'd be alive if they'd decided to have a beer instead of studying.

"But you can read all of this online. What you can't find is the exclusive information The Cadaver Hour *was able to obtain. One of the students, John Merill, was choked to death with his own backpack. Also, it seems the fish were biting, because John's face*

was partially missing. The poor boy's parents had to identify the body by a birthmark..."

After many made-up arguments, I arrived at my destination. The waving marsh grass on either side beckoned me to the once world-famous Crane Island. As I traveled the streets, I could almost hear the faint echoes of hooves on cobblestones as I imagined horse-drawn carriages transporting the world's most influential men from beach to hunting grounds to cottage. Would they cringe seeing the island so accessible and peopled by the shorts-wearing middle- and lower-class? I hated to admit it, but I'd fallen into this demographic, until recently.

Since I was a little boy, I'd always wanted to stay at the Crane Island Resort. Now, I was making enough money to afford a weekend. I was finally able to quit my job at the college since the podcast had taken off. Although working as the university archivist hadn't been horrible, it didn't exactly pay for the lifestyle I deserved.

I passed the ruins of the old Alexander Cottage. It seemed hollow and abandoned compared to the sepia image that was burned into my mind from pictures I'd studied. As I traveled the road that traced the coast, the boats parked in the marina bobbed as if begging for attention.

A vintage Ford Model-T greeted me as I pulled into the resort's grounds. A pair of gentlemen, clad in all white, knocked colorful croquet balls through wire wickets. I rolled my window down to get a clear view of the resort. The salt riding in on the breeze, blended with the scent of fresh-cut grass, reached out to me like an invitation. Gulls sounded their high, piercing call from rustling palm trees, much more serene than the pigeons and pine trees of midtown Atlanta. The club itself was an ornate tan building with a turret that reminded me of a sandcastle.

After parking in the adjacent lot, I approached the vintage car. The black doors, waxed to shine, reflected the club in a distorted image. Inside, the cracking leather was flaking off the seat and onto the floor. A thin layer of dust covered the dashboard.

I imagined myself sitting in the driver's seat when the car was new, taking in all the looks from jealous faces. When people would ask, "Where'd you get such a nice motor vehicle?" I'd reply, "If you have to ask, you can't afford it."

I stepped away from the car and lugged my suitcase toward the club. Once inside, the air conditioning embraced me like a cool blanket. I approached the front desk.

"Hello, sir, and welcome to the Crane Island Club Resort," the teenager manning the desk said with little effort.

His wrinkled slacks and basketball shoes showed me he had a few things to learn about professionalism. I assumed his parents, probably rich, got him his easy summer job. I couldn't understand why such a high-end resort entrusted him with the front desk when an older man, whom I assumed to be his supervisor, emerged from behind a door marked "Employees Only" in gold lettering.

"Hi," I said. "Checking in."

"What's the name?" the teenager asked.

"Henry Hall."

"Got you right here. You booked the...Dean Suite. Room 315. Third floor."

"You know your stuff."

A few clicks and keystrokes later, the teen handed me a gold key attached to a small rubber keychain. I looked down at his name tag.

"Thanks...Jake," I said. "Is there anything interesting about the Dean Suite? I read everything on the website, but I was just curious if there was anything else you could tell me."

The teenager glanced at his superior as if waiting for him to answer. The older man raised his palms toward me in a gesture that said, *"You know the answer."* The kid turned back and gave me his best customer service smile. I could see right through it, even if his teeth were perfectly straight. His braces must've come off not long before because he grinned each time it was my turn to speak.

"The room is spacious and beautifully decorated, complete with a large balcony. Only a few rooms have that."

"I already knew that," I said, matching his wide smile. "I was hoping you could tell me about the more...supernatural features of the room?"

"What?" Jake asked.

The supervisor stepped in front of the teen.

"I'll take it from here," he said, waving Jake away. "The suite does come with a chance to experience some unique phenomena. Do you read the paper by chance?"

"No," I laughed. "Unless it's on my phone. Or a podcast."

The man faked a laugh and said, "Well, George Dean, as you may or may not know, was a newspaper tycoon who stayed here from 1900 until his death in 1906. He occupied the Dean Suite and, after a few years, moved into the Jones Cottage down the road. Mr. Dean later sold his newspaper, *The Maine Gazette*, to what is now the *Canal Street Journal*. His paper reported on..." he looked at Jake, who was listening as close as I was. "...certain events that happened here."

"I've heard," I said. "Have guests experienced anything strange in that room?"

I knew the stories, but I was curious how much the resort staff would tell me.

"Yes. After he sold the *Gazette*, George Dean would ask for a copy of *The Canal Street Journal* and coffee every morning when he stayed here. These days, some guests bring their own copy of *The Canal Street Journal* to the room to inform George of current events. They say if you set the coffee and paper out and leave it unattended, you'll return to find the coffee cup half empty, and the newspaper disturbed as if someone has read it. Some have told us the room is ice cold, regardless of what the thermostat says. But I'll remind you all our rooms are perfectly safe."

"Of course," I said.

Some of the poor souls probably believed they'd been visited by a ghost. The cold room was most likely a clever excuse for the resort's outdated AC system.

"Any other questions?" the man asked.

"No," I said. "Thanks for explaining."

"You're welcome. We hope you enjoy your stay."

I nodded and walked to the nearby elevator. It seemed to be an antique. So antique I half-expected the cab to come with an operator. The gold doors reflected my image back at me. I appeared as a dark shadow and the checkerboard floors warped like a funhouse mirror as I shifted my weight from one foot to the other. The cab rattled as it arrived, and I took a cautious step inside.

After a quick ride up to the top floor, the doors parted and revealed a narrow hallway decorated with a patterned blue and white rug. I pictured myself in a past life walking down the hall, tipping my bowler hat to beautiful young women as they passed by. If I was lucky, I might've even glimpsed an ankle.

The suite was modest compared to the modern luxury hotels I'd stayed in. Each piece of furniture was made from dark-stained wood. Chairs, furnished with itchy red fabrics and flower patterns, surrounded a dining table in the corner alcove. On the opposite end was an antique desk. I hoped, but doubted, this was the same desk George Dean had used. The room's smell, a mix of flowers and lemon-scented cleaning spray, brought me back to my grandparents' living room. . The paint that covered the crown molding was chipped in places, reminding me of my first apartment in the city. A pair of white French doors led to a balcony overlooking the ocean. On top of the dresser sat a small plastic television that broke the historical fantasy.

I unpacked, then left my room to get a bearing on where I'd be staying for the weekend. Walking the opposite way down the hallway, I found a staircase behind a glass door. I descended creaking steps and exited the building onto a patio that wrapped around the north wing. It was half full of people eating dinner. Most of the men wore outfits that might've been appropriate for the golf course, but not a dinner. A fountain near the entrance sprayed water around its dirty bowl. It was a nice addition to the atmosphere, if you didn't look too closely.

I entered another section of the building and found a hallway with multiple doorways open on either side. The sound of clanking silverware and conversation made me feel as if I was missing the action. I regretted not putting on something more formal, but didn't feel like changing out of the T-shirt and jeans I had worn on the drive. Would these people be offended at the sight of me? I knew they'd be able to sniff the nouveau riche I reeked of. I didn't care. They were probably born into wealth anyway. Dinner parties and cigars were of no interest to me.

I peeked in each room as I passed and mostly found people, I guessed, in a lower tax bracket than I was. Guests kicked their feet up on leather chairs, played board games, and enjoyed their dinner in the glow of one of the many fireplaces in the lounge. At the end of the hall was a bar, empty for now.

I stepped outside and onto another patio, lined with white rocking chairs and small tables. It provided a great view of the ocean, foaming just beyond the tiled swimming pool. I would've loved to enjoy a cocktail and smell the briny air as it blew through my hair. The pool's turquoise water was not as still as I wished it was. Kids splashed each other and laughed, disturbing the serene feel of the resort.

I made my way to the opposite side of the pool and gazed at the resort's ocean-facing side. The pointed turret, striped with two balconies, would be the first of a few areas I'd report on. During preliminary research, I learned a few well-known ghosts were rumored to linger around the balconies as if the influential men, now wandering spirits, contemplated which direction the country should be steered.

A wide pathway lined the coast. I waited for two blue cruiser bikes to go by and then hopped on the path. A few workers were busy setting up for a wedding in front of one of the ancillary buildings. No ghost stories there.

Soon, I was in full view of Jones Cottage. It was even more decrepit than the pictures had me believe. The "cottages" on Crane Island were more akin to mansions the wealthy constructed as a getaway. The plaque to the left of the stone walkway that led to the building informed me of what I had already read online. It was constructed in 1903 after a wealthy doctor found the medical facilities of the resort lacking. His sick wife and dying daughter required near constant care and wide-open spaces. This was at a time when people believed illnesses could be helped with a little ocean air in the lungs. Unfortunately, the two succumbed to their illnesses, but some believed their spirit never left the building. George Dean didn't seem to mind, although his life also ended abruptly a year later.

Most cottages adjacent to the resort were kept up, and some were still used, but Jones Cottage remained a stone and wood shell. Another building I'd be reporting back on. I immediately began coming up with stories involving the family. Listeners would love to hear that their forms appeared to me and begged for help. Maybe they could even reveal something about how they really died. I'd need to be vague to avoid any risk of angry descendants...

My stomach growled and a painful pang twisted inside. I started back toward the resort, tinted by the sun's golden light.

I ascended the stairs, walked down the hall, and put my hand on the doorknob.

Ice cold. Was the AC broken?

I entered the room and shut the door behind me.

The icy air traveled into my lungs like chilled tea hitting a warm stomach. I shuddered and checked the thermostat. Seventy-two degrees. Was I getting sick? I couldn't be. The trip had just begun.

When I turned back around, a man stood on the other side of the bed.

A gold watch chain hung from the vest of his dark suit. He held a leather bag in front of him with both hands. His large mustache and pomaded black hair were both out of place and appropriate within the room's decor. Was someone playing a prank on me?

"I didn't ask for room service," I said.

"Very funny, sir," the man said.

"Who are you?"

"It's nice to see you back in your old room. We certainly outgrew this space, didn't we?"

I was silent.

"Will Mrs. Dean be joining you this evening?" the butler asked, raising his eyebrows.

"What?" I asked. "There's no Mrs. Dean here."

"Excellent," he said with a smirk. "Our usual spot in the ocean tonight, I assume?"

"I don't know what you mean."

"Of course, sir, very good." He winked, then said, "I'm pleased to see you harbor no ill will toward me after what happened. You must know, I did it to protect the both of us."

"After *what* happened?"

A burst of cold air hit me, making me recoil and shut my eyes. When I opened them, he was gone. The room's temperature returned to normal.

The world spun and I had to grab one of the bed posts to keep from falling. I paced around the room, half burning off anxious energy, half checking to make sure the butler wasn't hiding anywhere. The windows were secure. Could he have jumped off the balcony? The doors, locked from the inside, remained closed.

Did he think I was George Dean?

I confronted what I had just seen: a ghost. A real ghost. I wanted to run out of the room. As a kid I'd worried about catching ghosts in the corner of my eye. I believed every story I heard about haunted houses. As I grew, those beliefs went away. Anyone who actually believed in ghosts was being ridiculous. But I had no other explanation. My fingertips throbbed as my heart pumped high-pressure blood through my veins, sending pulsing waves of shock down my arms and legs.

In a panic, I grabbed a few of my belongings and ran to my car. I sped down the Crane Island streets toward home. My mind raced as I remembered all the times I thought I'd seen something. The voices I could've sworn I'd heard. Were those real, too?

My mind put the ghost interaction through one of my internal filters: money. Was there a way I could make money off this? I had an idea. I pulled over, picked up my phone, and called Kurt.

"Mr. Hall?" Kurt asked. His high-pitched voice made me think a woman had picked up the phone at first.

"Kurt. It's Henry. You won't believe what just happened to me."

"What is it?"

"I met one," I said.

"Met what?" he asked. "One of those older rich ladies you talked about?"

"No," I said "A *ghost*."

"Like an orb?"

"No, an honest-to-God formed spirit. Changed the temperature in the room and everything."

A pause. "You're messing with me again."

"I'm not!" I said, waving a hand like Kurt was there with me. "I promise on my life."

"Are you okay?" Kurt asked.

"I'm fine. It was just a butler asking me some odd questions."

"Wow," Kurt said, breathing into the receiver as if I had just met a celebrity.

"Listen," I said, "would it be possible for you to come down for the weekend? You're not busy, right?"

"Down to where you are?" Kurt asked. "With the ghosts?"

"Yes," I said. "You can help me record them. We'll put it on our website. Or sell the footage. Can you imagine how well this'll do? We'll be famous! And think of the sponsors."

"I don't know. They might be dangerous."

I rolled my eyes. "Oh c'mon, Kurt. Ghosts can't hurt you. The one I met wanted to go swimming or something. You'll be finc. I'll pay you time and a half."

"You don't pay me by the hour."

"Whatever," I said. "How about more airtime on the podcast? You could even do a segment or two by yourself."

"Maybe."

"Will you come?" I asked.

Silence.

"Kurt," I said as if talking to a child. "You owe me."

More silence.

"I'll come," Kurt said. "But remember I have to be back on Sunday for my sister's graduation."

"That's fine. When can you get here?"

"Maybe midnight."

"Perfect," I said. "We can start then. Bring microphones. And cameras."

I hung up and tossed the phone into the passenger's seat. Warmth blossomed from my stomach like I had just taken a shot of whiskey. This was it. We were going to become the most famous podcasters in the country. Maybe some of the most famous *people*. At least for a short time. But who was to say I couldn't keep it going? How long would people keep tuning in if they could see real ghosts?

I raced back to the resort and ran upstairs. The intoxicating excitement from the prospect of money made me barrel inside the room, unbothered by potential danger. It was empty of ghosts.

But I had to try.

"George Dean? Are you there?"

Nothing.

EXCERPT FROM THE CADAVER HOUR (ORIGINALLY RECORDED OCTOBER 8, 2023)

"... WE'LL GET RIGHT INTO it and start the show with our local crimes segment. We got hundreds of responses from those who enjoyed our insight on the Marie College killings. Well guess what? The killer was busy again. And like last time, we have exclusive information you won't be able to find anywhere else.

"But first, I think it's time we name this criminal. What do you think, Kurt?"

"Yeah."

"I'm so glad you agree. Ladies, if you're looking for a strong, silent type, then Kurt's your guy. Now, because these new killings occurred on campus again, a place everyone thought was safe, I think we'll call him the...Marie College Maimer. Is that a good name, Kurt?"

"Yeah."

"There it is. Remember, you heard it here first on The Cadaver Hour. *Now, you may be asking, 'Why did Hank choose* Maimer

and not something like Strangler?' *Well, our killer has evolved from simple strangulation to something a little more brutal. Another student, 21-year-old Greg Stillwell, was found dumped in the same campus pond as the Maimer's previous two victims. This time, however, the victim was stabbed. His torso and neck, dear listeners, were* covered *in one-inch stab wounds. I think it's safe to say there'll be a ten-foot fence around the pond after what happened to Mr. Stillwell.*

"And here's another detail the police won't tell you: the Maimer took Greg's ears. Cut them right off with the same knife, I'll bet. Maybe he wanted a keepsake? The start of a collection? Did he just want someone to listen to him? The only thing I collect are fridge magnets, but to each their own. One thing's for sure, it'll be a closed casket funeral.

"Now, I need to address something that's been brought to my attention. The police have denied my information from the last show. They say John Merill was not missing half his face. I'm sure they'll do the same with what I've told you today. Well, listeners, of course they'd say this. The police want to tamp down any hysteria the killings may cause. But you come here for the truth, and that's what you'll get..."

My stomach reminded me it was time for dinner. I consulted my phone and found a few shrimp restaurants in the area with good reviews. These would be off-limits when Kurt arrived. His sensitive stomach couldn't handle anything that wasn't boring and tasteless.

Once in my car, an indicator blinked for attention. The car's charge was lower than I realized. The closest charging station was twenty miles away. After my round trip to the restaurant, I'd have plenty of charge to get me there.

The short drive was pleasant enough, although a few clueless deer in the road made the trip longer than it needed to be. I pulled into the parking lot that served the small Crane Island Square and its few still-open businesses. After exiting the car, I spotted a closed liquor store; the amber bottles appeared golden as they reflected off the single dim light bulb, as if something ancient was held inside. Sand, deposited by the sandals and bare feet that had visited the nearby beach, scraped beneath my shoes. The ocean breeze blew my hair into a messy nest, and I finger-combed it back into place.

Two teen girls, whom I presumed to be the hostesses, chatted outside the restaurant's doors. How much of this island was run by children? They directed me to an open table, but I opted for a single stool at the end of the bar. I scanned the sticky menu and, before I could decide what I wanted, a tall woman about my age walked over. Her red bandana matched her ginger hair and flushed face. But she wasn't bad looking.

"Can I get you anything to drink?" she asked.

"Yes," I said. "Let me get the..."

The five draft handles displayed breweries I had never heard of. The one closest to me would do just fine. At least there were some craft beer options.

"I'll have the hop...the hop one," I said, giving her a polite smile.

"That won't do," she said, grinning. "I ain't gonna give it to you if you can't say it."

I read the handle again.

"The Hop...Dang-Diggity. Please."

"You got it. My daddy comes in here and says 'Gimme that Hop Dang!'"

Another rough-looking patron at the other end of the bar laughed, exposing missing teeth.

"You don't make Daddy say it?" I asked.

"What's that?"

"Nothing."

The beer was better than expected. I ordered a basket of Georgia shrimp with a side of hush puppies and fries. Most of the men sitting around me were either overweight or dirty or both. There weren't any women who warranted a second look aside from the crass bartender, although I had to remind myself I was getting up there in age, and once you hit thirty, your dating options became limited. There was usually a good reason why someone was still single. As for me, I was too focused on work. A healthy relationship requires time and effort. I was doing myself and the women a favor.

I couldn't imagine spending my Friday nights there. The man a few seats down took a bite of his chewy steak and slapped it back down on his white, chipped plastic plate. Did they look forward to this all week? If any of these people were handed a menu from my favorite restaurant in Atlanta, they wouldn't recognize a single item.

I couldn't blame them. They didn't know any better. I could've been in their place if my family had made a few worse decisions. Although my situation could've been better, too.

After one beer, my mind wandered back to the hotel room. Could there have been any rational explanation for what I'd seen? A trick played by my brain? I was overworked, sure, but it wasn't as if a shadow had darted away from the edge of my vision. The butler *responded* to my questions. Kurt's presence would help. Another set of eyes, along with recording equipment, would be able to confirm I wasn't going crazy.

The tall woman came by and refilled my glass. The head of foam left my upper lip tingling. The second one went down smoother than the first.

I finished my meal and second beer, the tall woman looking better with each sip. She came over, took my glass to refill, and smiled at me. She might not have been wife material, but they didn't all need to be.

"What's your name?" I asked.

"Charlotte," she said.

"You like working here, Charlotte?"

"Could be worse," she said, shrugging.

"Anything fun to do on the island? I'm only here for the weekend."

"There's the beach, of course," she said. "Or you could rent a bike."

"What do you like to do?"

Her eyes flicked to the other end of the bar. A hairy arm raised an empty glass, and she walked away.

I felt stupid. When Charlotte finished serving a few more patrons, she stood on the opposite end of the bar, fidgeting with glasses. Can't give up that easily. I raised my hand and got her attention.

"Yeah?" she asked, raising her eyebrows.

"How are you doing tonight?"

"Listen, I don't have time to chat," she said, taking a few steps away from me.

"Sorry," I said to the back of her head.

Anger burned hot in my stomach. I finished my third beer, embarrassed. The drink cooled me down. She wasn't worth getting upset over. She probably had a husband anyway. I glanced at her bare third finger. She probably took it off before her shift. I stared at Charlotte until her eyes drifted my way. I raised two fingers and mouthed the word "Check." She brought it over and I took it without making eye contact.

"What're you doing here this weekend?" she asked.

I looked up. Her eyes were elsewhere. Just a practiced question to ensure I tip her.

"Ghost hunting," I said, hunched over, inspecting the bill.

"Really?" she asked.

I looked up again, but this time her eyes were on me, and her lips curled into a half-smile.

"Yes," I said, sitting up straight.

"If I were you, I'd check the pier. The one by the resort. You know where that is?"

"That's where I'm staying."

"Then it'll be a short walk."

"Thanks."

"Anytime, hon," she said, walking away.

I left her a generous cash tip and wrote my number on the check, just in case.

It was a short drive back to the resort. Late nights of podcast research had strengthened my alcohol tolerance, so I was fine behind the wheel.

By my estimate, I still had about three hours until Kurt's arrival. I couldn't think of anything else to do besides go back to my room. Drinking should stop for the night. I didn't want to be hammered when Kurt got here. We had work to do. I'd go back to my room, maybe make a phone call, maybe scroll on my phone. If anything, a nap would do me some good. Although I doubted I could fall asleep in that room after what had happened. We had a long night ahead of us if the ghosts were out to play.

Once parked, I ignored the lobby's attractive energy and headed straight to my room.

As I stood in front of the door, I was unable to open it. I told myself the butler's appearance was nothing more than an opportunity for fame and money, but I froze when confronted with the possibility there was a ghost on the other side.

I removed my phone from my pocket and started recording a video. At least this way, I wouldn't need to look directly at a spirit if one showed itself. Also, I didn't want to miss a chance to catch a ghost.

I held the screen up to my face and reached for the doorknob.

Cold again.

But not as cold as last time. I told myself it was just the natural chill of the metal in the air-conditioned hallway.

I opened the door, but, through the phone, the room was black. A low hum reverberated in my bones as I took a wary step inside. My ears popped. I stood in silence for a bit to steady myself. A few seconds passed before I tapped the phone screen so the camera would focus somewhere inside the room and adjust to the low light. As it did, I caught sight of something in the corner.

A woman.

"Hello?" I said, taking a step forward.

"Why are you doing this?" she said, her voice breaking.

My phone shook in my hands. It was difficult to make out any specific details about her. She wore a long dress and large hat. It looked as if she had a fruit basket on top of her head.

"Doing what?" I asked. "Who are you?"

I took another step forward.

She raised her hands in front of her, as if shielding herself from me.

"Stop, George! Please!"

She began to scratch at the walls.

I expected to hear her nails against wood, but the room was silent.

"I'm not going to hurt you," I said.

"You're a monster!" she yelled.

To show my harmlessness, I moved away from her. I zoomed in with my phone's camera.

She screamed.

I flinched.

Her hands lowered to dark spots blossoming on her dress. Blood? More blotches appeared, her screams becoming quieter and quieter until they were grunts. Soon, she slumped over and was motionless.

"Hello?" I asked.

I steadied my breathing, and looked out from behind my phone, still pointed in her direction. Something acidic rose from my stomach and I forced myself to swallow it back down. The smell of iron filled my nose. I moved toward her unmoving body.

A cold wind blew into my face, and I instinctively protected my chest.

She was gone.

I stopped my phone's recording and stood still in the dark room.

The second ghost encounter left me less shaken than the first. I was more concerned about what I had just seen. Who was that woman? Why did she think I, or George, was going to hurt her?

I watched the video back. It was dark, but the ghost was visible. I couldn't wait to post this on the podcast's website.

My heart sank when I reached the end of the recording. Right before the spirit disappeared, the camera was not on her. It had jerked away when the air hit me.

I debated uploading the video. All it showed was a terrified woman cowering away from the camera and my voice. The stab spots were visible, but who could be sure those weren't from a gun? Even without a body or a death reported, the rumors would circulate. Someone could say I changed the time of the video and blame me for the murder of any woman killed on or near Crane Island. I was almost sure I couldn't be convicted, but it'd hurt the podcast.

Or would it?

Any attention is good attention, and I wasn't exactly trying to be a role model on the show.

I still had more than two hours before the real ghost hunting would begin, so I lay down and turned the television on. I propped my phone up on top of the bed's headboard and started a video recording to catch any activity that may occur if I dozed off.

Blessed with a talent for falling asleep in almost any situation, it only took me about ten minutes to start feeling sleepy. Plenty of guests over hundreds of years had stayed in this room. If the ghosts hadn't hurt them, they weren't going to hurt me. I told myself this over and over again until I drifted off.

Excerpt from The Cadaver Hour (originally recorded November 1, 2023)

"... We have an exciting show today, but I have to warn you, some of the details are hard to listen to. So, I'd advise you to grab a pair of headphones. You don't want others to think you're a freak, do you?

"The monsters and ghouls were out last night, but there was only one that was truly dangerous. The Marie College Maimer was celebrating Halloween and two students, let's just say they didn't need a costume to look horrifying by the end of the night.

"Ryan Lowell and Connor Polk were found this morning about a hundred feet from a Marie College apartment where a Halloween party was held. The student who found them reported that at first, he thought they were just passed out. But when Ryan and Connor didn't wake up, he knew there must be some real blood mixed with the fake stuff.

"The two business students were both dressed as undead golfers. Real original. I'd hazard a guess they just threw on some preppy

clothes, a mask, dashed a little fake blood on their faces, and called it a day. Me, I like to go all out on Halloween. Last year I was a mob boss and the year before that, Elvis.

"When police removed the students' masks, they discovered both sophomores, like Greg Stillwell, were missing their ears. The Maimer's collection is growing. Is he keeping them in jars? Does he dry the ears and sew them onto something?

"One thing I do know, two sets of parents got the biggest scare of their lives this morning.

"And I'd just like to remind our listeners that your host, Hank Blight, is dedicated to the truth. I'm willing to go the extra mile. I attended Greg Stillwell's funeral. It was very touching. I even shed a tear. However, Kurt was stone faced. Unemotional. Isn't that right, Kurt?"

"Well, I wouldn't say—"

"But I'll tell you the most important thing: Greg's casket was closed. Exactly as I said it would be. How else do you explain that?

"Now, back to the most recent crime. One of the victims, Ryan Lowell, was particularly brutalized. Twice as many stab wounds as Connor. Mostly in the neck. They had to be careful when removing Connor's mask, as to not remove his head in the process..."

I WOKE UP TO my phone ringing. When I opened my eyes, my hands were pressed together and resting on my chest, as if I had been praying. My feet had been pushed together. I sat up and scanned the room. Empty. I picked up my phone, stopped the recording, and answered Kurt's call.

"Hello?" I asked.

"Mr. Hall...Henry...I'm here. In the parking lot outside the resort."

"I'm coming."

I pocketed my phone and exited the room. The sun had sunk below the oak trees, draped with gray Spanish moss, and the resort felt livelier than it had during the day. Like it was nocturnal. Loud conversations, no doubt greased by alcohol, made the walk much noisier than I would have liked.

Kurt stood outside his car. He gave me a wincing smile as I approached his dented sedan.

"Thanks for making the drive. Did you bring cameras and microphones?"

"I did bring some good microphones. The ones you had me buy when we were planning to do an episode on-location."

"Great. What about cameras?" I asked.

"Well...I only brought one," Kurt said, looking away. "But it's my roommate's camera. We need to be careful with it. It's expensive."

"Why didn't you run to the store and buy a couple new ones?"

"I don't really have the money for that, sir."

"You don't have the money for it?" I asked. "Did you ask your parents? They certainly have a few hundred dollars to spare."

Kurt's family, the Greenes, had an incredible amount of money. I wasn't sure what it was Kurt's parents did to earn their wealth. I've asked Kurt, but all he says is something about logistics and owning warehouses.

"I didn't ask my parents," Kurt said. "But there's a microphone on the camera. And we each have our phones."

"That'll do for tonight. Maybe we'll go to the store tomorrow."

I turned to walk back to the resort.

"Mr. Hall?" Kurt asked in the loudest voice I had heard from him, which wasn't very loud at all. "Can you help me bring my stuff in?"

"What stuff? The equipment?" I asked, peeking into Kurt's car.

"Yeah. And my suitcase."

"Your suitcase?"

"I thought I was staying with you. Is that all right?"

I hadn't given Kurt's need for a place to stay any thought.

"Are you sure you want to?" I said. "I've already seen two ghosts in my room. I may have caught more on video while I was sleeping."

Kurt looked at his shoes and then over my shoulder toward the resort behind me.

"I don't have any other option."

The idea of a relaxing weekend to myself was crashing down, but if we succeeded, I'd have more luxury weekends ahead of me.

"Fine. Follow me."

For the second time that day, I wheeled a suitcase toward the Crane Island Resort. In the dark, the turret made the building look more like a haunted castle than one made of sand.

"Wow," Kurt said as the hotel came into full view. "This place is incredible."

"You'll have time to explore tomorrow. Tonight, we need to focus on capturing some ghosts."

"Right."

"Let's start with the room. We need to drop this stuff off anyway."

We took the creaking elevator up and soon stood in front of the door. Kurt and I took out our phones and began recording. I put my hand on the doorknob.

Normal temperature.

I swung the door open, and we both stepped inside.

Nothing.

Kurt whipped his phone in every direction. I turned on the light.

"No ghosts," I said, stopping my video recording.

Kurt exhaled as if he had been holding his breath. My phone vibrated. Only ten percent battery left.

"Let's move to the next location. I need to leave my phone here to charge. You take the big camera, and I'll use your phone."

"Where are we going?" Kurt asked.

"The Jones Cottage."

"Can we even go in there? Isn't it closed?"

"The worst they can do is kick us out," I said.

Kurt grabbed the camera, and we headed out into the cool summer night. The sounds of laughter and jazz music accompanied us as we moved along the ocean path.

We crouch-walked to the rear of the Jones Cottage. Luckily, the building's doors had been removed, so entry was not difficult. However, this meant any light we shone would be visible from the outside. I hit the red record button on Kurt's phone and was pleased with how well it did in low light. Not everything was visible, the darkest corners of the room still hidden, but it was the best I had.

"We can't have any light, or someone could see us from the outside," I said.

"Gotcha," Kurt whispered.

A bright light lit up the cottage, blinding me for a moment. A camera flash.

"Sorry," Kurt said. "I don't know how to work this thing. I think I just took a picture."

"What did I just say? Figure it out!"

Maybe bringing Kurt was a bad idea.

Kurt fiddled with the screen until he was satisfied. He began recording.

"How's it look? Can you see anything in the dark?"

"Yes," Kurt said.

"Give me one of the microphones."

I held out my hand, but all I heard was Kurt patting his pockets.

"I forgot them," Kurt said.

"What?" I said.

The fizzy anger in my stomach, the same anger I had experienced at dinner, returned.

"Do we need them?"

"Are you asking me if we need microphones for an *audio* podcast?"

"We can just use the ones on the—"

"Go!" I said through gritted teeth.

I wasn't convinced we did need them, but I wanted there to be consequences for his mistakes. Maybe he'd remember this moment and never forget any equipment again.

Kurt disappeared into the darkness, and I heard footsteps brush through the grass.

I waited and pointed Kurt's phone in each direction. I didn't want to progress through the cottage without every piece of equipment available and it was only midnight, so we had plenty of time. As I spun, the dust under my feet scratched with every step. Bare walls and ceilings, all the same gray color, were the only things visible on the screen.

The room was silent. I held my breath.

The pressure in the room shifted. My ears popped.

There was something in the room with me. My eyes hadn't perceived it yet, but my bones and nerve endings did.

"Father says you killed us," said a child's voice from a dark corner.

I pointed Kurt's phone toward the sound.

"Who's there?" I said, my voice almost a whisper.

"He says we'd be a happy family if you would've left us alone," said the voice, this time from a different part of the room.

I didn't respond.

A figure moved in the corner of my eye.

I turned and hid behind the phone screen.

A little girl, sitting in a wheelchair furnished with wood and wicker, emerged from the darkness. Her chair looked more like something you'd see on a southerner's porch. The wheels creaked with each turn. Where was Kurt?

"Who are you?" I asked.

"I'm Rose."

"Are you a ghost?"

"I don't know," Rose said. "I don't feel like one."

She looked down at her lap and then to her arms.

"Are you?" she asked.

"No," I said. "Why...why are you here?"

"I don't know that, either," Rose said. "I thought we left this place. Father said we had to get on the train and go back home. Because of you. I was so tired."

I zoomed in with the camera. Her sunken cheeks and dark eyes were barely visible. She wore a baggy dress and buckled shoes over high white socks.

She paused, then said, "I should be asking you. Father said you made us leave, Mr. Dean."

She thought I was George. I wanted to tell her I wasn't him, but I also wanted the clip.

"You had to leave, Rose," I said.

"I know, Mr. Dean. But I'm glad Father brought us back. Everyone here is so wonderful. Especially the maid."

I approached her. If Kurt wasn't there, I wanted to get as much content out of this as possible.

"What are you doing?" she asked, squirming in her wheelchair.

"I just want to see you," I said.

"Stop. Please. Go away."

Rose's frantic voice nearly made me stop. She grabbed the wheelchair's wheels and turned them, easing her backward.

"Father," Rose said. "Help me."

I took a few quick steps in her direction. She sank into the blackness behind her.

I reached out.

A calloused, scabbed hand emerged from the shadows and grabbed my wrist.

I looked up into the clouded eyes of a man. A dark streak ran across his neck as if it had been slit and drained.

"You!" the man yelled.

My insides felt as if they had fallen to the floor. I tried to pull away, but his grip only tightened.

I screamed.

"Mr. Hall!" someone said behind me.

It was easy to recognize the high-pitched voice. Kurt's voice.

I turned and looked over my shoulder. Kurt's dark figure stomped toward me.

"What's wrong?" he asked.

I looked straight ahead, but the hand and face were gone.

Excerpt from The Cadaver Hour (originally recorded November 8, 2023)

"...Our local serial killer was busy again last night, just a week since the last pair of victims. Is the Maimer's thirst for blood becoming more ravenous? If he keeps up this pace, we could have a murder victim every day! However, this time, he didn't just murder. Forty-two-year-old Helen Grier, a tenure-track Professor of Education, was found in three pieces. Where he was unsuccessful with Ryan Lowell, he completed his task with Dr. Grier. That's right, add dismemberment to the list of the Maimer's crimes. The professor's head and right arm were separated from the rest of her body.

"And the Maimer did not give her the courtesy of removing these body parts after death. He took her back to his lair, tortured her, and dumped her body right onto Marie College's quad. The students who were on their way to class early that morning even saw the fingers wiggling. I guess that means the legs went first. As you know from yesterday's podcast, she'd been missing for two days

before being discovered this morning. What did I say? I knew she would become the Maimer's sixth victim.

"Now, here's where it gets even tougher. Helen had two young children. A five-year-old named Mia and a seven-year-old, Becca. Very cute kids. Dr. Grier would bring them to campus regularly. I sure hope they don't listen to this podcast. Even worse, I'm told Tim Grier, the children's dad, recently lost his job. Now that Mom is gone, who is going to provide for their daughters?

"Dr. Grier's funeral is this Saturday, November 11th. I hope anyone in the area will attend to pay their respects.

"Now onto the sponsor for today's show..."

"What happened?" Kurt asked. "I was only gone for a few minutes."

I couldn't move. My legs felt like they weren't there. The ghost had *touched* me. I looked down and rubbed my wrist, but there was no mark.

What was Rose talking about? George Dean forced her and her family out of the cottage? The butler had said something about outgrowing the old room.

"Henry," Kurt said, startling my focus back into the echoing room.

"Yeah?" I responded, a little annoyed.

"What'd you see?"

"A little girl. She was in a wheelchair."

"Where is she?" Kurt asked, bringing his camera up to his eye.

Good question. I knew whatever force was with me a moment ago was gone. It had been there during the last two ghost encounters, to a lesser extent. Sounds came rushing back that had receded during Little Miss Ghost's visit. The ocean waves.

The gentle hum of the resort next door. Feet dragging against the floor.

"They vanished when you came in," I said.

"They?"

"I also met the little girl's dad."

"Did they hurt you?"

"No. You showed up just in time."

Kurt may have saved me. Do they only appear when I'm alone?

"What do you mean?" Kurt asked.

"The ghost grabbed me, Kurt. They can interact with the real world. You must've scared them off."

"What? They can *touch* you? I'm not staying in that room, then."

I had forgotten about that. I didn't want to stay in that room either after what I had just experienced.

"Can we leave?" Kurt asked while shuffling his feet and looking around the room. "Go somewhere else and talk?"

My silent bones assured me no more spirits were present, but I also didn't want someone to find us trespassing. However, I couldn't resist messing with Kurt a little.

"Why?" I asked. "Are you scared?"

I wasn't sure if Kurt could see my smile in the dark room or not. Either way, I tried to hide it.

"No," Kurt said. "I just don't think we should be hanging around here longer than we have to."

"You're right," I said. Then louder, "Oh my gosh, what's that?"

"What?" Kurt said, panicked.

"On the floor!" I yelled.

"What is it? A rat?"

Kurt's scuttling feet sent me over the edge. I bent over, laughing. Kurt's feet stopped moving and I heard him let out a long sigh.

"I'm sorry, buddy," I said between wheezes. "I was kidding. Let's go."

Kurt didn't respond, but I could feel him trying to stare a hole into my head.

We exited the cottage through the back and made our way inside the resort. First, we tried the lounge, much too loud this time of night. Why did a few drinks make everyone speak as if there was no one else around? We found two rocking chairs on the patio facing the ocean.

"All right," I said. "I'm guessing you don't want to sleep in that piece of crap car of yours. So, we need to find a hotel."

"Can we find one open this late?" Kurt asked.

"Of course. Let me look—"

My phone.

I patted my pockets as if it would materialize in one of them.

"We need to go back to the room. My phone is still there."

"Do you need it?" Kurt asked.

"Yes, Kurt. I do."

I could be away from my phone for a few hours, but the thought of being without it, cut off from the world, for the entire night, made me anxious. What if I got an urgent phone call? Also, I wanted to go back to the room to test a theory I had.

Kurt got up from his chair, causing it to rock back and almost hit the wall behind it.

"I don't want to go back in there," Kurt said. "You said the ghosts could touch you."

"Listen, Kurt. It'll be fine. I'll be with you, all right? I know when ghosts are around. I can feel it. If I sense anything weird, we'll turn around and use your phone to find a hotel."

Kurt stared at me, his eyes flicking back and forth between my left and right eye.

"You can feel it?" he asked. "How?"

"It's hard to describe. When the spirits are around, my ears pop. My bones vibrate. It feels like my body is humming. I know it's odd but trust me."

"Okay," he said, nodding to himself. "Let's be quick."

We walked up the stairs and down the hallway. Kurt moved slow, like he was a death row prisoner approaching the electric chair.

I put my hand on the door.

Nothing. My bones and nerves were quiet.

"There's no ghosts, Kurt. It's safe."

I opened the door and flipped on the light. I took a few steps inside, leaving Kurt in the hall, and scanned the room.

Empty.

"See?" I said, sticking my head back out into the hallway.

Kurt nodded and entered the room.

"Why are there no ghosts now?" Kurt asked.

"I don't think they appear when you're around. Think about it. I've only seen them when I was alone. We didn't see any in the room earlier. They vanished when you came back to the cottage."

Kurt relaxed his shoulders.

"So, they won't show up if I'm with you?" he asked.

"That's my guess."

"Okay. That's good. There'll be no ghosts if I sleep in the room, right?"

Kurt was proving more useful than I had anticipated. He might've just saved me a few hundred bucks in hotel bills. But my theory was only that, a theory. Was I prepared to put it to the test? Would I be able to sleep in this room anyway? I had done it earlier today.

The video.

"I took a video earlier," I said. "When I was napping. Let's see what I got."

I sat down on the bed and Kurt joined, a little too close, and I moved a few inches away. The video was almost two hours long. I hit play.

The camera angle only showed me from the waist down. I scrolled through the timeline. The first hour was uneventful.

Just an empty room in the daylight. As the natural light drained away, the bathroom kept the room partially lit. In one dark corner, the blackness stirred. It bulged and stretched.

The butler emerged.

"Who is that?" Kurt asked.

"It's the butler from earlier."

"My goodness. What's he doing?"

"Shush," I said.

In the video, the butler stood over me, crying. He took out a handkerchief from his jacket pocket and dabbed under his eyes.

"God, forgive me," the butler said. "And I hope you do too, Mr. Dean. It's time to let the ghosts sleep."

The butler then bent down and, out of frame, moved my body. He picked up my legs by the ankles and pressed them together. This must've been why I woke up as if I had been in a coffin.

The butler vanished in full view of the camera.

The rest of the video was uneventful. It was almost more unsettling that way. My body was completely vulnerable to whatever the ghosts wanted to do with me. Even though I knew I was safe, I couldn't keep my eyes on the screen.

"What did he mean by 'forgive me?'" Kurt asked.

"I don't know. But I suspect it has to do with what he told me earlier."

"What'd he tell you?"

"He said something about protecting the both of us. It sounded like he did a horrible thing to George Dean, and he was happy George wasn't mad at him for it."

"What was he doing to you?" Kurt asked. "Did he hurt you?"

"I'm fine."

"Good," Kurt said, getting up from the bed. "I guess it doesn't matter what the butler was talking about. We have our ghost footage. He vanished into thin air!"

"Yeah..." I said as my eyes stared into space.

I couldn't leave. There was more work to be done. More answers to find.

"Great," Kurt said. "Can you send me the video so we can—"

"We're not leaving," I said.

"What? Why not?" Kurt asked as if he were a child who never heard the word "no."

"I need to find out what happened. I need to know why I wasn't given the life I deserve."

"What does any of this have to do with you?"

It was time to come clean. I needed to stop lying to myself about why I came to Crane Island. Why I was so interested in staying, despite the danger.

And Kurt had to stay, too. He owed me.

"George Dean was my great-great-great-grandfather," I said.

Excerpt from The Cadaver Hour (originally recorded November 13, 2023)

"...As I'm sure everyone is aware, the Marie College Maimer has been apprehended. I'd like to remind everyone the Maimer name that's been appearing on every Atlanta news station and radio broadcast was coined by me, Hank Blight. Make sure you tell anyone who brings it up you heard it here first on The Cadaver Hour.

"Our neighborhood killer was back in full force last week, adding two more victims to his body count for a total of eight, each one missing some or all of their face.

"Thirty-one-year-old Jim Upton, a resident of the Poplar Park neighborhood, is being charged with two of the murders. Many think they got their man. That the streets are safe once again. Everyone has breathed a collective sigh of relief.

"But I'm here to tell you the truth. Jim Upton is not *the Maimer. He can't be. Mr. Upton is barely five and a half feet tall. Greg Merill was over six feet tall and on the baseball team.*

There's no evidence, except circumstantial, that proves Upton did anything. No murder weapon. No collection of severed facial features. No taped confession. Yes, he was seen with the victims. Witnesses say he bragged about taking 'spoiled college kids'' lives.' But I'm here to tell you the real Maimer is still out there. More killings will happen. I'm sure of it..."

"George Dean?" Kurt asked. "You're related to *the* George Dean?"

"I am," I said.

"Why isn't your last name Dean?"

"I'm related to him on my mom's side. Dean is my middle name. She wanted to keep our connection to George alive, no matter how weak."

I pulled out my ID and handed it to Kurt.

"Henry Dean Hall," Kurt read aloud. "I can't believe it. Why didn't you tell me?"

I was hoping Kurt wasn't going to ask that question. But I suppose it was inevitable. Growing up, telling people about my relation always led to follow-up questions I didn't have the answer to. Why isn't your family rich now? Why's your house so small? I learned to just keep the information to myself. People were never as impressed with my connection to George Dean as much as I thought they would be anyway.

"Why would I?" I asked.

"We just did a whole podcast episode on Crane Island, and we mentioned Mr. Dean...George...quite a bit."

"Well, Kurt, if you remember anything from that episode, you know he didn't pass his wealth on to anyone in the family. He sold the newspaper right before he had a heart attack and died. No one knew where the money from selling it went. His kids were left on their own."

"Right," Kurt said. "Amazing."

He looked at me as if I were royalty. His mouth hung open and curled up in a slight smile on the right side. It made me uncomfortable, but I did enjoy the admiration. I just wished it came from someone else. Where was this appreciation when I was a kid?

"Stop looking at me," I said.

"Sorry," Kurt said, turning away. "It's just a lot to take in. Do you think he knew Eileen?"

"I doubt George knew the names of any of the maids who worked at the resort."

Eileen was Kurt's great-great-great-grandmother. Kurt learned, after talking with his parents, that Eileen had worked at the Crane Island Resort around the same time George Dean was there. Kurt's five-year-old great-great-grandmother was left with just one parent after Eileen succumbed to health complications from a nasty accident she suffered the same year George died.

"You're right," he said. "So, you want to know why none of George's money made it to you?"

"That and why the ghosts keep blaming George for terrible things."

"What terrible things?" Kurt asked.

"The little girl in the wheelchair said George kicked her out of Jones Cottage. She said that's why she died."

"I thought she died *in* the cottage," Kurt said.

"I did, too."

"Huh," Kurt said, staring into space. "Anything else?"

"That's it."

It was best, for now, to keep the encounter with the woman in the big hat to myself. Perhaps I wanted to protect George. More likely, I wanted to convince myself George didn't hurt anyone.

"So, where do we start?" Kurt asked. "Should you try to talk to the butler some more? Or go back to Jones Cottage?"

Solid ideas. However, at that moment, I wanted to rest. It wasn't late, at least for me, but there wasn't much more I could do that night. I didn't want to go back out looking for ghosts, especially now that I knew they could hurt me, without taking further precaution. I doubted I could find any protection at this hour, physical or otherwise.

"We'll worry about that tomorrow," I said. "I'm not going back out there like this. Let's call it a night and get an early start in the morning."

"Sounds good," Kurt said.

I knew he'd be receptive to staying in. He sat back down as if I had just removed a weight from his shoulders.

"Where will I sleep?" he asked.

"On the floor," I said.

"But the bed is huge. I promise I'll stay on my side."

He was right. The bed seemed to be even bigger than a king size. The floor, although carpeted, was hard and cold. I had slept in the same bed as one of my brothers growing up, and I doubted Kurt would be as bothersome as he was.

"Fine," I said. "But put some of the extra pillows in the middle."

Kurt and I got ready for bed and turned out the lights. I lay under the heavy comforter on my left side. The soft glow under the door reminded me the resort never really slept. My mind tried to chew on the day's events, but my tired body and the warmth of the sheets put me right to sleep.

Since 1879, the Crane Island Resort has been the preferred getaway for those seeking the elegance and refinement of home while overlooking the beautiful Atlantic Ocean. Our beachfront resort features all the comforts you've come to expect, including fine dining, a full bar, expansive grounds, spa services, an experienced medical team, and so much more!

Saturday, June 8, 2024

I WOKE TO THE same feeling I had my first morning in college: disoriented and confused about my surroundings. My mind expected to see the morning sunlight casting a window frame watermark onto the beige walls of my condo in Atlanta. I could almost hear Rambo pawing his kennel door. Instead, the popcorn ceiling and Kurt's snore, just like my college roommate's, greeted me.

I went through my morning routine and as I got dressed, Kurt woke up.

"Good morning, Henry."

"Morning."

"Where are you going?" he asked, sitting up.

"I'm going down for breakfast. The resort is supposed to have one of the best in the state."

"That sounds great," he said with a sigh. "I brought some crackers. I'll probably just eat that."

I didn't particularly want company, but I wanted the kid to enjoy his time here.

"Get dressed. I'll buy your buffet ticket," I said. "I want you fueled up for the day."

"Really?"

"Yes. See? I'm not a bad boss."

Kurt jumped out of bed. I sat on the recliner in the corner and waited for him to get ready. After I had read a few news articles, Kurt stepped out and told me he was good to go.

The main dining room was something to behold. Two of the largest chandeliers I'd ever seen hung from the coffered ceiling, seemingly held up by six wide Roman columns evenly spaced throughout the room. The chafing dishes, each silver and spotless, wafted the heavenly smell of butter and bacon to my nose. Each table and chair were seemingly designed to impress nobility.

We were seated and I was disappointed to find my chair wobbled just a hair. I ordered coffee and Kurt asked for orange juice.

The food was just as good as it smelled. Buttermilk biscuits that disappeared under sausage gravy, thick bacon, and some of the softest eggs I had ever eaten filled me up in a hurry. I wished my stomach was bigger. Kurt and I ate in silence, despite his questions. I told him I couldn't think straight before a few cups of coffee, but really, I just wanted to enjoy the meal in peace. Thinking about what was ahead of us that day would've distracted me from the food on my plate. Warm French toast and a third cup of black coffee rounded out one of the best meals of my life.

"All right," I said, throwing my napkin on top of my empty plate. "It's ten o'clock now. Why don't you go find me some protection against the ghosts. I'll go to the electronics store to look for cameras. Let's meet in the lobby around noon and go from there."

"What kind of protection?" Kurt asked.

"Something physical. I don't want the ghosts to be able to touch me."

Kurt nodded and then said, "Henry? Would it be okay if I borrowed some money? I just paid my rent and I'm a little light. You can take it out of my next check."

"That's fine."

I wasn't sure how much to give him, but I knew heavy clothing, pads, and a helmet could get pricey. However, my safety was worth every penny. If I wanted to be protected, I'd need to pay up for it. I handed Kurt three crisp hundred-dollar bills.

"Is that enough, you think?"

"It's plenty."

Kurt rubbed the bills like he had never had that much money in his hands before.

"Good. Bring me back the change.."

"Will do," Kurt said. "See you later, Henry."

I paid the bill and walked to my car. The low-charge indicator blinked for my attention again, but the closest electronics store was only on the next island.

As I passed the Crane Island sign that welcomed visitors, I felt the urge to flee. I couldn't help but stare to my right, toward the highway that could lead me back home. To safety. But as a car approached from behind, I took a left.

When I arrived at the store, a man, much too old to be working his job, asked me if I needed help. There was no way he could help me as much as online reviews could, so I politely waved him away.

I opted for a full-frame camera, a point-and-shoot, and a tripod. Since the ghosts could only appear to me, I didn't need to get Kurt a camera. I figured I could set up the bigger camera on the tripod to film the entire room and I could easily wield the point-and-shoot.

Next, I needed a way to communicate with Kurt in case it got too dangerous. We could've used our phones, but I wanted a backup. Something reliable. I grabbed the only pair of walkie-talkies the store sold.

Lastly, I put a pair of battery-powered flashlights in my cart as well as some batteries.

I checked out and drove back to Crane Island. I had a half hour to kill before meeting back up with Kurt, so I decided to enjoy the resort as much as I could. This trip didn't all have to be about ghosts and the podcast. I bought a soda from the lunch counter and sat on one of the patio's rocking chairs facing the ocean, my purchases sitting beside me on the table. The book in my suitcase would've made a welcome addition, but I didn't feel like going back to the room alone. Instead, I opened the cameras and familiarized myself with the controls and settings. I'd need to head up to the room to charge the batteries, but that could wait.

"Hey, Henry!" Kurt said, making me jump. "You weren't in the lobby, but I found you."

"Great," I said. "Is it noon already?"

"It is," Kurt said. "Did you get some cameras?"

"I did."

"Awesome. I did well, too."

Kurt held a single grocery bag with various items stretching the plastic at the bottom. There was no way there was enough in there to protect me from dangerous spirits.

"What'd you get?" I asked.

"Well, you wanted protection, right? I went to a local crystal shop. The owner was a woman who called herself a Wiccan. I'm not sure what that means. Anyway, she gave me all this amazing stuff. Sage to cleanse, obsidian to protect your aura, selenite to provide spiritual insights. No way ghosts can touch you with these."

I should've been clearer about what I meant by "protection." Also, how did Kurt not know what a Wiccan was? Perhaps he was underqualified to be on the podcast.

"I hope you kept the receipts," I said.

"Of course. Why?"

Maybe Kurt was right to take this approach. Two days ago, I hadn't believed in ghosts at all. Now, everything was on the table. I'd give the stones a shot. I put the obsidian and selenite into my pocket. But I wasn't leaving my life in the hands of some rocks.

"Never mind," I said. "Where's the change?"

Kurt handed over much less money than I thought he would.

"How much did all this cost?" I asked.

"It was only fifty bucks, but I needed to fill up my gas tank, too. I hope that's all right."

"You didn't think to ask me first?" I said with a little more edge than I intended.

I had no problem with Kurt spending my money for gas, but it hinted at future unacceptable actions. If I didn't say anything here about it, he could take advantage of me later.

Kurt rubbed his elbow, then said, "I just...figured because it was part of the job to drive down here...gas would be covered."

"You figured? I don't pay you to figure, Kurt. I pay you to do what I say."

"I'm sorry, Mr. Hall. Henry. I'll pay you back."

"Thanks. That's very kind of you."

Kurt sat in the rocking chair next to mine and stared down at his lap. We stayed in uncomfortable silence for a minute or two.

I wanted him to stew in his own embarrassment. But not too long. I still needed him to be on my side during the trip.

"Hey, Kurt," I said, putting my hand on his shoulder. "It's all right, you don't need to pay me back. Just ask me first next time."

"Thanks, Henry," he said, laughing to himself as if he had just dodged a bullet. "It won't happen again."

"Great. Now, come up to the room with me so I can get these cameras charging and then let's enjoy the resort a little, huh? This trip doesn't all have to be serious."

Kurt looked up.

"What'll we do?" he asked.

"Have you ever played croquet?"

Excerpt from The Cadaver Hour (originally recorded December 15, 2023)

"...That concludes our local crimes segment for today. Will the missing persons covered today turn out to be Maimer victims?

"Speaking of the Maimer, we have had some reports come out this week about the supposed killer, Jim Upton. He's taken credit for all the Maimer's victims. But he hasn't provided any information that proves this. I think Mr. Upton's statements are purely a fame grab. He knows he'll be spending the rest of his life in prison. Why not try to go down as one of the most famous criminals of the last fifty years?

"Jim Upton just wants to grab some last-minute attention while he still can. It's disgusting if you ask me. In fact, if I could, I'd pay to have him sent to the chair today. Instead, my tax dollars, and yours, are being wasted keeping a convicted killer alive for who knows how long.

"Anyway, thanks again to all our dedicated listeners for tuning in during this somewhat uneventful period. Things will pick up here soon. I know it..."

Once the camera batteries were charging, Kurt and I headed to the lobby to grab croquet equipment.

The middle-aged woman behind the desk smiled at me, one of her front teeth smeared with lipstick. It seemed like a genuine smile, which somehow made me more uneasy than if it had been forced.

"Good afternoon," she said. "How may I help you?"

"I was looking for the croquet equipment. Do we get that here?"

Her mouth remained stretched in a smile, but her eyes lost their joy. Instead of squinting, they opened wide as if she was grinning through pain. In a fraction of a second, she scanned me from head to toe. Kurt and I weren't wearing all-white like those guys had been when I arrived at the resort. Was there a dress code?

"Of course," she said.

She ducked behind the desk and handed over two mallets and a canvas bag.

"Thanks," Kurt said.

Once outside, I spilled the multi-colored balls onto the manicured lawn.

"Do you know how to play?" Kurt asked.

"Not really. I assume you just hit the balls through the wickets."

Kurt proved to be a natural. I'm sure with more time to practice I could've beaten him, but that day, I was overmatched.

Saturday was a busy day for the resort and there were many people (not guests, I assumed) walking around and taking pictures of the resort. About halfway through our game, a pair of older women stood just outside the field's boundaries, holding what looked to be their personal croquet set, and stared at us. Their crossed arms signaled they were less than patient with us. One woman's white clothing contrasted against her tan skin. The other's pale complexion nearly matched her outfit.

Kurt smacked a ball through one of the wickets and pumped his fist. An impressive shot. I looked at the women for their reaction.

The pale one said something to the tan one, pointed and shook her head. Were we playing wrong? I tried to ignore them. They could wait for as long as it took for us to finish. They'd do the same if we were waiting.

After the game ended—Kurt handing me my ass so badly I wanted to shove the mallet up his—we walked toward the two women who were between us and the lobby. Their eyes hid behind sunglasses, but I still felt their judgmental gazes.

"How'd we look out there?" I asked the tan woman.

"You certainly hit the ball hard enough. First game?"

"Yes," Kurt said. "Sorry if we—"

"Something wrong with how we played?" I asked.

"Not necessarily," the tan woman said. "There wasn't much finesse, though."

"What's it matter if we score the same amount of points?"

"It doesn't. But your mistakes will be much worse than if you were a little more...thoughtful. Delicate."

"Well, neither of us is planning on turning pro," I said, starting to walk away.

"Clearly," the other woman said, and both laughed.

I stopped. My cheeks burned.

Kurt put his hand on my shoulder and guided me away from them.

"Let it go, Henry," Kurt said.

I breathed deep and put one foot in front of the other.

After a quick stop in the lobby to drop off the croquet equipment, I asked Kurt to go back out and find some real protective equipment. I made sure to be specific this time: arm and leg padding, thick clothes, and some kind of helmet. I wasn't too concerned about being completely covered as I knew the ghosts would vanish as soon as Kurt walked into the room.

While he was away, I went back over my notes from the Crane Island podcast. I wanted to make sure we were hitting all the potential ghostly sites. We could've gone back to the Jones Cottage or our room, but I didn't think we could get any more answers out of the butler, and I was done talking to dead little girls.

My research proved to be surface level. The show notes on my computer had many blank spaces to be filled with made-up ramblings. None of the information that wasn't written down was true, so listening to the episode would be useless. Also, many of those podcast sections had nothing to do with Crane Island at all. I remember going on about adjacent topics. I hadn't even looked at old newspaper articles from when the Crane Island killings took place.

A few sites granted me access to *The Maine Gazette* newspaper articles from just before George Dean sold it. I hadn't covered a lot of the details in the podcast, but I had marked down dates, which made it easy to find what I was looking for.

The newspaper ink was blotchy and faded in spots, but the text was still legible. The edges of the pages looked burned and torn as if it were charred with a lighter. It reminded me that digging this deep was a pain in the ass.

The Alexander family, who owned the Alexander Cottage I had passed on my way to the resort, were some of the unfortunate victims of the Crane Island Killer. The newspaper article from the day after their death mentioned a few interesting details. Walter Alexander and his seventeen-year-old son, August, had been visiting the family cottage for a summer hunt when they were both found floating in the ocean foam. George's newspaper didn't shy away from mentioning parts of both of their faces had been missing, likely from being fish food. Walter's and August's portraits, framed in thin ovals, featured their matching strong jaws.

A quick internet search informed me the Alexander Cottage was one of the oldest structures in Georgia and the Alexander family helped found the colony that would later become Georgia. Also, the family cemetery, where Walt and Augie were buried, was in the building's backyard.

Some of my grandfather's old photos showed the Alexanders and Deans posing outside the resort. Maybe Walter could give me some answers. I was sure they were well acquainted.

Gossip spread just as fast back then.

Kurt returned with more or less what I had asked for. A baseball helmet, football forearm guards, and soccer knee pads would do nicely. I wished the baseball helmet had a face cage, but it was the best they had, Kurt said.

We opted for an early dinner and went back to the room to change.

"Where are we going?" Kurt asked.

"We're going to the Crane Island Ocean Club. The sister resort on the north part of the island. Put on the best clothes you brought. It's a nice place."

"I didn't bring my fanciest clothes," Kurt said, glancing at his open suitcase.

"I'd offer to let you borrow some of mine, but I don't think they'd fit. Just put on whatever you have."

I dressed in a suit I had brought for the occasion. I hoped Kurt had at least brought pants, but when he emerged from the bathroom in a short-sleeved collared shirt and shorts, I contemplated getting his food to go. But, like breakfast, I wanted him to experience some fine dining. Most of his dorm room dinners probably came from the microwave.

"How's this?" Kurt asked.

"It's fine. Next time bring pants."

When we arrived at the ocean club, the hostess, an adult this time, sat us at a candlelit corner table. I blew out the candle.

I felt out of place the moment I walked in. Even Kurt was overdressed. Since the restaurant was attached to a hotel, many were in swimsuits and sandals. Didn't they have any respect for the restaurant or themselves? A man at the bar with hairy feet and yellow toenails almost made me lose my appetite. More than a few people stared at us as we looked over the menu, making it hard to figure out which cut of steak I wanted. Did they think Kurt and I were on a date? I asked for a cocktail, making sure to pick a respectable whiskey. Kurt got a soda.

During dinner, Kurt and I discussed what I had found that day about the Alexander Cottage.

"Are you sure we should go there?" Kurt asked, pushing his mashed potatoes around his plate. "A man and son sound more dangerous than a butler or a child in a wheelchair."

"It'll be fine. If anything happens, I yell, you run in, and they're gone."

"I'll make sure I'm ready."

We finished our meal and drove back to the resort. To avoid any unwanted non-ghost visitors, we'd wait for the sun to go down so the Alexander Cottage would be empty.

Kurt and I headed up to the room to kill time. I was hoping to get some of my thoughts down to prepare for the podcast episode that would come out of this experience. Maybe one of the biggest episodes of all time, backed up by *real* ghost footage. I grabbed my laptop and sat on the balcony, looking to soak up the pink sunset. There was a second chair next to mine but, with any luck, it would remain empty for a while.

The first thing I did was check my bank account to make sure the most recent sponsor check had come in. It was still hard to believe a sixty-second ad read could earn $100,000, more than I used to earn in two years working for the college. I knew the money wouldn't be coming in like that forever, but after this weekend, I wondered if I could start spending my earnings a little more freely. Maybe I could take another look at that penthouse.

Next, I checked the Atlanta news to see if the Marie College Maimer or its investigation made any headlines. Nothing.

I opened the notes application on my computer and titled the document "The Big One." I'd just begun typing the first sentence when Kurt popped his head outside.

"Can I join you out here?" he asked.

"I'm busy, Kurt. You can sit, but I need to focus."

"I'll be quiet," he said as the balcony creaked under his bare feet.

He sat in the rocking chair next to mine. Out of the corner of my eye, I could see Kurt adjust his position, scan the resort grounds below, then start humming while occasionally looking over at me to see what I was doing.

"Would you mind moving your chair to the other end of the balcony?" I said.

"Sure."

He picked up the chair and moved about ten feet to my right.

After another five minutes, I had only written a few sentences about the weekend, just bullet points of my encounters thus far. I missed my home office where I could block out all noise. The birds and waves and Kurt's presence made it almost impossible for me to write anything that took concentration. I shut my laptop.

"Are you done?" Kurt asked. "Can I ask you a question?"

"I'm done. What's up?"

"What was it like growing up, knowing you were related to George Dean? Did you tell everyone about it?"

"I didn't think about it too much."

In all honesty, it was frustrating. I should've had more than I was given and other kids at school made sure I knew it. I grew up in a rich area of Atlanta in a non-rich family, which meant I never had friends over to my house, the few I had at all. Thrift store clothes and past-generation electronics made me an easy target. My friends played video games that ran on consoles we couldn't afford. Whenever I wanted anything, my parents reminded me it would be coming out of my college fund. For Christmas and birthdays, I asked for things I didn't want, but thought would make me fit in. Kurt's question picked at the scar tissue I hid these memories behind.

But learning about George Dean gave me hope. He grew up with even less than I had. He started his newspaper with almost nothing and completed each step of the process himself. He wrote, printed, distributed, and sold each issue for the first few years. He stood on street corners shouting that day's headlines even after the issue was available in nearly every newsstand. I knew I had that potential.

And that potential, however small, was given to me by my mother. My dad reminded her and me every chance he got that the family would've been rich if George Dean hadn't squandered the family fortune. I agreed with him, but it wasn't my mom's fault we were poor. It was his. He had more opportunity than George ever had and did almost nothing with it. Success was as much about spiting my dad as it was about living the life I was owed.

I tried everything I could afford. I started blogs, YouTube channels, accounts on every social media available, and my own news site, which was quickly shut down due to copyright reasons. Even *The Cadaver Hour*, my first real success, was the fifth podcast I had started since high school.

I kept my real name hidden from the podcast audience because I knew my dad would ask me for money if he found out how rich the show had made me. My mom knew and was nothing but happy for me. She never asked for a cent.

"Henry?" Kurt said, interrupting my drifting thoughts. "Are you okay?"

"I'm fine," I said. "Just thinking about work."

"Have you ever thrown your relation to George Dean around? Did it get you into fancy places?"

"People only care about who you're related to if there's money behind it. Hardly anyone even knew the Dean name. Even fewer cared."

"Maybe they would now," Kurt said.

"I doubt it. No one knows me by my real name anyway. People probably care more about yours than mine."

Kurt's family would've put all the kids who made fun of me to shame. Instead of living on a golf course, the Greene family had one built on their property. It was only three holes, but still, it was impressive. I was invited to dinner at Kurt's parents' house every once in a while, and each time was an amazing experience. I'd stare at the high ceilings and huge rooms and wish I had grown up there.

Kurt's father could've gotten him a cushy internship, but even Mr. Greene couldn't deny how valuable the experience would be for his son to work on one of the most popular podcasts in the country. His resume will stick out from the crowd quite easily, and Kurt's father's connections aren't as valuable for Kurt's chosen career path. He wants to start a show of his own.

I told him good luck. It takes a special talent to be able to entertain millions of people each day.

"Well, I think it's pretty cool," Kurt said.

"Thanks."

At least one person was impressed.

"What are we going to do until it gets dark?" Kurt asked. "We still have two hours."

"I don't know. Any ideas?"

"We could watch a movie," Kurt said, his voice rising in excitement.

"I'm not watching one of those Japanese horror movies you like so much."

"I don't want to watch one of those either. Too many ghosts here already."

"How about a comedy?" I asked.

"Sounds great," Kurt said, getting up.

Once back inside the room, Kurt pulled up a chair and turned it toward the small television on the dresser. I lay on the bed.

Excerpt from The Cadaver Hour (originally recorded December 25, 2023)

"...Very exciting news today, loyal listeners. It seems the Maimer was busy again. A Marie College student was robbed on campus last night. Eighteen-year-old Connor Inman told police the masked man shouted 'Maim' over and over again while fleeing the scene with the student's belongings. The laptop and phone were found dumped in the same pond where the first two Maimer victims had been found, but the student's wallet remains missing.

"This comes just two days after a pair of students were horrifically attacked while walking home from the campus library. Why aren't these kids at home for Christmas? Do they not get along with Mom and Dad? Both women are expected to fully recover from their injuries, but the knife wounds left a mark all Marie College students are feeling. No one feels safe anymore. Following the attack, the school's administration advised all students to be home before sundown.

"As a reminder, The Cadaver Hour *will be posting new episodes through New Year's. We don't take holidays off. And from our listener data, neither do you..."*

As the movie's credits rolled, I got up from the bed and turned on the lights. The sun had gone down, taking the light inside the room with it.

"Should we...get ready to go?" Kurt asked.

"Let's do it," I said.

I got dressed, fitting the shin and arm guards under several layers of clothes. I grabbed the helmet to put on when we got to the cottage.

Kurt grabbed the shopping bag from the electronics store and stuffed it with the cameras, walkie-talkies, and a lapel mic. We exited the resort and got into my car. Kurt noticed the low-charge indicator as soon as the engine turned on.

"Do you have enough to get us there and back?" he asked.

"Yes," I said. "Plenty."

"Should we just take mine?"

"I'm not riding in that thing."

Kurt was silent. The Alexander Cottage was about three miles away, far enough off the main road that I wasn't worried about anyone stumbling onto our ghost hunt.

"Crap," Kurt said. "My phone's dead. Can I plug it in?"

"What? You knew we were going to need it. Why isn't it charged?"

Kurt squirmed in his seat.

"I didn't notice," he said. "I'm sorry. We can use the walkie-talkies."

"At least one of us is prepared."

Kurt connected his phone to the outlet.

During the drive, Kurt fidgeted in his seat and asked questions that had nothing to do with Crane Island or my family history. It came across as a nervous distraction, but I welcomed it.

My car's tires skidded as I came to a stop in the small gravel parking area in front of Alexander Cottage. The car's headlights threw the trees' shadows against the stained white exterior. It reminded me of a rotting, dead tooth. Shattered windows with jagged edges looked like they could cut to the bone. In the dark, it appeared to me as the subject of an urban legend. I imagined local kids daring each other to knock on the front door at night.

As if sharing my unease, Kurt said, "Should I stay in the car? So I don't interfere with the ghosts?"

"Yeah, that's the reason," I said, laughing to myself.

The baseball helmet was a tight fit, most likely because it was meant for teenagers. I killed the engine, fastened the mic and walkie-talkie to my hoodie, and grabbed the two cameras. After exiting and locking the car, I shut off the headlights. I switched on my flashlight, which meant only part of the house was visible to me. It was worse that way. I flipped the beam to each glassless window, hoping they would be empty.

As I approached the cottage, my bones vibrated more and more with each step. There was something inside. By the time I was at the front door, I wanted to turn around. But Kurt was watching. I reached for the doorknob.

"Henry." Kurt's voice vibrated the walkie-talkie on my chest, making me jump.

I pressed the button and said, "Yes, Kurt?"

"Good. I was just checking that you could hear me."

"Loud and clear," I said. "If you don't hear from me in five minutes, come inside."

A pause, then, "Roger."

I shone the flashlight against the wall above the door. It seemed to be made of shells and sand. Like it was constructed from the ocean itself.

I set up the larger camera on its tripod, hit record, and positioned the flashlight under the point-and-shoot. I pushed open the door and stepped inside.

This time, I didn't hide behind the camera screen. The room was empty, but a faint hum rang in my ears. There was no furniture. Nothing hanging on the walls. Just an empty room in a crumbling structure.

I walked around the lower floor, hearing and seeing nothing, but sensing I wasn't alone.

"Hello?" I said, the walls bouncing my words back to me.

Nothing.

"Walter Alexander? Are you there?"

Nothing. Maybe they'd respond to an old acquaintance.

"It's me, George Dean... Your friend."

My ears popped.

"You're no friend of mine!" said a raspy voice from above me.

The voice sent a wave of shock though my body, tingling each nerve ending. I looked up, but there was nothing but shadows. The camera shook in my hands. The helmet's padding became wet with my sweat.

After steadying myself, I asked, "What did I do that was so wrong?"

"Why don't you come up here and I'll show you."

I knew I shouldn't go upstairs. My flight response was trying to yank me out the door. But I had to know. If he could tell me why George's money was taken from me, it was worth the risk. Kurt would be close behind, anyway.

"Okay, I'm coming up."

A wet laugh boomed down from the upper floor, rattling my bones and swelling the hum in my ears. The gurgling sound made me think Walter had liquid in his lungs. I proceeded until

I found steps that led to the second floor. In one quick motion, I turned and pointed the light and camera at the top of the stairs.

Nothing.

I could hear feet squelching above me.

"Henry?" Kurt said through the walkie-talkie. "Are you okay?"

"I'm fine. Give me another few minutes before you come in."

"Got it."

The first step bent and creaked under my weight. I pointed the flashlight at my feet in case any steps were broken. When I reached the top, I kept the flashlight down. I knew if I saw him, I'd want to run without any answers. The stairs were right behind me if I needed an escape. I took a breath and steeled myself.

"Walter?" I asked the dark room.

"Yes?" Walter said, his voice bubbling as if water was spilling out with each word. "What can I do for you, George?"

"Can you tell me why you're upset with me? I'm wondering why my money's all gone."

"You know what you and that butler of yours did to me and my boy. Killed us in our own home. All for a headline."

"I'd never do that, Walter. You know me."

"All too well I'd say. I only hope you repented."

The voice was getting closer.

"You said your money is gone?" Walter asked.

"Yes," I said.

"That's the best thing I've heard in years," Walter said, laughing. "You got exactly what you deserved, you rat."

The familiar anger boiled in my stomach, but this time, I couldn't keep it down.

"You're lying!" I yelled.

I flipped the flashlight and camera up into the room.

Walter's face was a few feet from mine. His black, water-bloated body and half-missing face almost made me drop the camera.

"Killer!" he screamed through what lips he had left.

He punched the camera into my right eye, causing me to drop it and stumble backward. I turned and ran down the stairs.

I was almost at the bottom when the last step broke, and I felt something scrape hard against my shin. Behind me, Walter laughed, his wet feet slapping the stairs as he came toward me. I yanked, but my foot was stuck.

Closer.

My foot knocked against the splintered wood.

Closer.

I grasped my leg with both hands and pulled.

A wet hand grabbed my shoulder.

I jolted at Walter's touch and sprang free. I made for the closest door, the one that led to the house's backyard. It was hard to tell how hurt my leg was, but the cool air stung my skin a little more where my shin had scraped against the wood and tore my pants. My right eye throbbed with every heartbeat.

I took a few steps outside and turned back toward the house. I began to walk backward and catch my breath. The sensation that I was near a ghost lessened but didn't disappear. A nervous laugh escaped my lips.

My heel knocked against something jutting up from the lawn, and I landed on my ass. The helmet fell off and bounced away. I pointed the flashlight at what had tripped me.

It was August Alexander's grave marker.

I looked at the two dates. Only seventeen years apart. I thought about all the life I had lived since I had turned seventeen. All the life I still had ahead of me.

I felt something grab my heel.

"Killer!" A wet voice said from behind me.

I ripped my leg free and shined the flashlight at where the voice came from.

August's ghost creeped out of his grave. The ghost ripped up the grass as it fought to get close to me. It grunted and breathed heavily.

It freed itself.

"Kurt!" I yelled, scooting backward.

August crawled toward me on all fours. I tried to stand up, but he caught up to me in an instant.

August grabbed my bad shin. Sharp pain surged through me, and I howled.

"Kurt! Help!"

August moved farther up my body until we were face to face. There was no skin left from the cheeks down, and his teeth chattered as he looked at me with lidless eyes.

The ghost grabbed a handful of my shirt with his left hand and reached back with his right, preparing to strike.

Even without lips, August smiled.

He brought his fist forward, and my vision went black.

Kurt shook me as I woke from what felt like an hour-long dream. Like most of my dreams, they made no sense. Just flashes of hallways and empty rooms.

"Henry!" Kurt yelled with both hands on my shoulders.

I groaned at the pain in my face and shin.

"Are you okay?" he asked in a panic.

"How does my eye look?"

He shined the flashlight into my eye, making me put my hand up to block the blinding light.

"It looks fine. Maybe a little red. What happened?"

Kurt's presence made the panic inside my head go away. For the first time in my life, I felt like someone was looking after me. As if someone in the world genuinely cared if I was safe. The hum inside my body was gone. My bones were silent. There was no more threat.

"I met the Alexanders. Neither gave me...or George a warm welcome."

"Are you hurt? You were knocked out. I almost called 9-1-1, but you woke up right away."

"I might have a black eye. And my leg is cut up. I might lose it."

"What?" Kurt said, shining the light on my leg.

"I'm kidding. I'll be fine."

"You sure you're okay? Do you need to go to the hospital?"

"I promise I'm all right. Better than all right, actually. I got some great video. Help me up so we can get going."

Kurt pulled me to my feet, and we walked into the house, its energy drained with Kurt next to me. My leg was scraped, but I hadn't lost any strength in it. I was more worried about it being infected than seriously hurt. The broken stair must've torn the shin guard right off. Money well spent.

Kurt walked upstairs after a bit of convincing and retrieved the broken camera. I hoped the memory card was still usable.

I fetched the big camera by the front door and stopped the recording. At least one device made it out alive.

"So, you said I was only out for a little bit? What time is it?"

"I don't know," Kurt said.

"You don't have your phone?"

"It's still charging in the car. I heard you scream and rushed out as fast as I could."

I stopped walking.

"You haven't unplugged it yet?" I asked in shock.

"No," Kurt said in a hushed voice.

I ran the few steps back to the car and got in. I pushed the start button.

Almost out of battery.

"Get in!" I yelled.

Kurt jumped in and unplugged his phone. I sped away from Alexander cottage. There was less than a mile left of charge, but I hoped there was some grace period. Like when a gas car goes a little past "empty" on the indicator. It was only three miles back to the resort.

There was no grace period.

Shortly after turning onto the road that lined the coast, the "gas" pedal no longer responded to my panicked presses.

The car slowed and I coasted onto the shoulder. It came to a halt, and I took a long breath out.

Kurt and I sat in silence for a few moments.

"I'm so sorry," he said.

It was an honest mistake. A stupid one, but it happens.

"It's fine," I said. "Let's just focus on getting back."

"I'll walk to the resort and pick you up in my car."

He put his hand on the door handle.

"Wait!" I shouted, surprising even myself. "I'll come with you."

"Your leg is hurt. And this is my fault."

"True. But I could go for a walk on the beach."

I didn't want to be left alone after what had just happened at the cottage. It was unlikely another ghost would show up, especially inside my car, but I didn't want to take that risk. Not now. Plus, maybe a walk would take my mind off what the Alexanders had told me.

I removed the arm guards, extra layers of clothing, and the one shin guard I still wore and left them behind. The helmet, I realized, I had forgotten in the Alexander's backyard. That was fine. Ghosts seemed to go more for the face and neck than the head anyway.

We got out of the car and began down the path, the ocean's waves creating a steady rhythm I might've enjoyed if I wasn't stranded.

"What'll happen to your car?" Kurt asked. "You can't fill a gas can with electricity."

"I'll get it towed to the nearest charger."

"Oh," Kurt said. "Will it be expensive?"

"It won't be cheap."

"Does the resort have a shuttle? Or do you want to call the tow place now?"

"The shuttle just goes back and forth between the resort and the ocean club. And the tow truck will take forever. I want to get back so we can go out again. It's only a couple miles."

"We're going back out?" Kurt asked, his voice now rising. "After what just happened?"

"Yes," I said.

"Why?" Kurt asked, stopping.

I stopped too and faced him.

"Because I need to know what happened here!"

I didn't want to tell Kurt that Walter Alexander accused George of being a killer. He'd look at me in a different light.

"Did Walter Alexander give you any more information?" he asked.

"Nothing helpful."

"Where do we go next?"

"Let's just get back to the resort and we'll figure that out."

We walked in silence. The gentle chirp of bugs would've been welcome ambience if it wasn't for the mosquitoes. The vision in my right eye began to narrow. It was swelling. I knew from childhood fights I'd wake up the next morning with a black eye. Every five minutes or so, a car would pass on our left, and I was glad when they didn't stop. The ride back would come with annoying questions I didn't feel like answering.

After about a half hour of walking, I needed to use the bathroom.

"Keep walking," I said to Kurt. "I'm going behind the bushes. I'll catch back up."

"All right," Kurt said.

I waited about ten seconds before taking a few steps into the tall grass. When I finished my business, I looked out into the ocean. The blackness stretched on forever. Walter Alexander's accusation returned to me.

Was George the Crane Island—

There was something floating in the water.

I squinted. No, it was two things. One in the ocean and one where the beach met the water.

"Help!" A voice came from the figure near the water.

I didn't think twice. I ran straight through the wispy grass and onto the beach. On the sand, it felt as if I was running in a dream. It took a lot of effort to go a short distance, and I kept stumbling.

When I arrived at the two figures, one was on their knees with their back to me, holding the other as if they had just found a body washed up on the beach. The person on their knees looked to be a man wearing a suit.

"Do you want me to call 9-1-1?" I asked as I approached.

"What are you talking about?" the man said in a choked-up voice.

"Are they okay?" I asked, taking a few more steps closer.

I looked over the man's shoulder.

He held a woman in a maid's outfit who looked to be unconscious. She had wounds that stained her outfit red. They looked like the blotches on the woman's dress from my room on the first day. The one I had gotten a video of.

"Oh, Eileen," the man said.

"Eileen?" I asked.

Kurt's great-great-great-grandmother? *That* Eileen?

I crouched and put my hand on the man's arm.

In an instant, he turned to face me.

"Killer!" he yelled as they both disappeared.

I sat on the sand and stared into space, trying to wrap my head around what I had just learned. George had tried to kill Eileen. Kurt's entire family was changed because of what George had done. A pang of guilt hit my stomach, but vanished when I remembered how well off Kurt's family was. Maybe George did them a favor. What did Eileen do once she recovered? Did she tell the police? Nothing in my research mentioned George was a murderer. I figured this was because none of the victims survived. But one had. Eileen's injuries, the ones that ended her life years later, were inflicted by George. Or were the ghosts lying?

"Henry!" Kurt shouted. "Where are you?"

"Here!" I yelled back. What was I going to tell him?

He made his way to me, struggling just as much as I did, and crouched down.

"Are you okay?" he asked. "Why are you on the beach?"

"I...thought I saw something."

"Did you?" he asked.

"No," I said. "It was just a piece of driftwood."

"Where?" Kurt asked, looking around.

"Never mind. It floated away."

We both got up and walked back onto the path. The remaining trip to the resort was quiet enough for my head to focus on Eileen's ghost. George's greed affected someone I knew. As much as I didn't want to admit it, I cared for Kurt. He was as much a friend as I had. He drove all the way down to Crane Island at my request. I did strong-arm him into it, sure, but he still came. At every point, he asked if I was okay. He cared about my wellbeing more than anyone had before.

After twenty minutes we spotted the soft glow of the resort on the horizon. The splotch of civilization was a welcome sight after traveling in the darkness. We immediately made our way to the room, all the while keeping our heads down to avoid any unwanted attention my condition might've attracted. I looked like I had just lost a street fight, which was almost true.

Once in the room, I washed my leg and filled a bag of ice for my eye. August must've clipped me right in the chin because there was a small red mark there, which explained how he knocked me out with one punch. After about fifteen minutes, I felt better. I tried talking Kurt into going back out. He was resistant. Scared.

And I was, too. August and Walter's attacks could've ended much worse. If Kurt hadn't found me, who knows what August would've done to me? Maybe a drink would help calm the nerves. It would at least numb some of the pain from my leg and head.

"Listen, let's stop at the bar before going out. We can think about it. Talk it out. After that, if you still don't want to go out, we won't."

"I don't drink."

"I know. I'll buy you a soda. Don't you want to sit at the bar? I heard some famous people drank there."

"Fine."

I wondered if Kurt was only agreeing to procrastinate going back out. He probably hoped I'd get drunk and forget about everything.

The bar wasn't as busy as I expected. In the corner, the grandfather clock chimed, its bronze face showing 11:30, half an hour before closing time. Glass bottles stood in front of their reflections atop carved dark shelves. Backless barstools, studded with brass buttons, were tucked underneath the semicircle bar top.

There were more than enough stools for Kurt and me, but any hope of having a drink unnoticed was gone. My swollen eye was bad enough to catch some glances. An older woman whispered to her husband and they both looked up at me from their leather recliners. With any luck, they'd think I was someone not to be messed with. But, most likely, they thought I was an idiot who fell off his bike or got hit with a stray croquet ball.

The bartender came over and took our orders. The menu included an assortment of drinks from different decades of the resort's history, from the 1880s to the 1940s. I ordered a "Prohibition Daiquiri," and Kurt got a Shirley Temple.

When the bartender returned, he said, "If you don't mind me asking, how'd you get that shiner?"

"Ghost hunting," I said. Kurt flinched to my right.

"Is that right?" he asked. His smile told me he thought I was joking.

"Of course," I said, playing along. "You know they run this place."

"I do indeed," he said.

An unexpected response. Perhaps he could point us to our next location.

"Do you have any ghost stories?" I asked, trying not to sound eager.

"Yes, sir."

"Would you mind telling us? They might help our search." I faked a laugh to make sure he thought I was joking.

"I will," he said, then looked over his shoulder. "But only because it's slow tonight. Wouldn't want to scare anyone away."

"Of course not," I said.

The bartender started, "One night, we had a particularly lively evening at the bar. I think they were having a wedding on the grounds the next day. Anyway, I was cleaning up the glasses and heard a voice from behind me. It asked, 'Barkeep? Can I take a drink with me?' I turned around and there was a beautiful woman standing there in a gorgeous red dress. Fiery red hair to match. She looked straight out of the early aughts. Big hat with flowers on top, a sun umbrella, the whole thing. I didn't think much of it. People come here and pretend they're old money all the time."

I took a sip of my drink. Was he talking about the same woman I saw yesterday getting stabbed in my room?

"I said, 'Of course, ma'am. What'll it be?' She said, 'As long as it's got whiskey, I'm a happy girl.' I made her a drink, an Old Fashioned, and asked, 'Would you like to charge it to the room?' She said, 'Yes. Only, I'm not sure which room that would be.' I asked, 'Why's that?' She said, 'I'm a guest of Mr. Dean.'"

I gripped my drink tighter.

The bartender continued, "She said, 'He's invited me here. Something about a job at the newspaper.' I didn't know what to say. I knew who Mr. Dean was. Part of the job requirement is knowing the resort's history. I thought I'd just play along. I said, 'I'll take care of it. What's your name, miss?' She said her name was Florence. Florence Gibson. She thanked me for the drink and just as she reached for it...she disappeared." The bartender punctuated this last detail with a wave of his hand and wide eyes.

I stared at the man, waiting for him to continue.

"I thought it was weird, you know? So, I look up this Florence Gibson. And guess what I find? She was murdered! They found her body washed up on a beach not far from here. I saw it in an article in *The Maine Gazette*, some newspaper that isn't around anymore. Isn't that strange?"

"Very," I said. "Quite the story."

"But here's where it gets even stranger. One day I went into the Dean suite after a guest checked out. I noticed the room was ice cold. And then, I'm bending down to restock the mini fridge, when suddenly, I hear: 'Help me!' right in my ear! I looked around and there was no one there. The bathroom was empty, too. Can you believe it?"

"No," I said. I finished my drink with one gulp and pushed the empty glass away.

"It's true," he said. "They never found out who killed that girl. But you know what I think?"

I knew what he was going to say. Who was he to make such bold accusations? He probably just told himself all successful men were bad people to make him feel better about his situation.

"I think that's enough—" I started.

"It was George Dean!" he said, turning a few heads.

"You think?" I asked, rubbing my eye.

He shrugged, then said, "I wouldn't be surprised. Most of the men back then, especially the ones who stayed here, had some dark secrets."

"You don't know what you're talking about!" I yelled, drawing stares from the few people that had joined us in the lobby.

Kurt stirred in his seat.

"I'm sorry," I said. "I think you made that last drink a little too strong. I need to head back to my room. Can I have the check?"

The bartender gave an uneasy nod. He probably guessed my black eye had something to do with my temper. After taking a few drink orders from newly arrived patrons who didn't know how to wait their turn, he handed me the bill.

"Just write your room number and name and it'll be charged to your room."

I did and moved toward the door with Kurt following close behind.

"What was that about?" Kurt asked.

We walked onto the deserted patio that faced the ocean. I thought some fresh air would calm me down.

"Sorry," I said.

"Do you think it's true?" Kurt asked. "Could George Dean have killed that woman?"

"I don't know."

"But if he did, why would he do it?" Kurt asked.

"Probably to sell more papers," I said.

"Kind of like—"

"Wait," I said.

There was a figure at the end of the pier. It looked like a woman, her long hair blowing in the ocean breeze, with her back to us. She stared out into the blackness beyond the sea. I had forgotten Charlotte's advice. She had told me to check out the pier at night. Was I seeing another ghost?

"Do you see that woman?" I asked Kurt, pointing to the figure's faint outline.

"Yes," Kurt said. "What about her?"

"Stay here," I said.

I approached, my feet knocking against the creaking wood planks that stretched over the salty water. If it was a ghost, why was it still visible with Kurt around? My scraped leg throbbed when I imagined one of the slats breaking and removing more of my flesh. As I neared the figure, they turned, and I saw a familiar face.

"Charlotte?" I asked.

"Hey there," she said. "I see you took my advice."

"I did," I said. "I thought you were a ghost."

I took a few more steps toward her.

"I know I'm pale, but—hey, what happened to your face?"

"Oh, this?" I touched my swollen eye. "I got into a little scrape."

"Are you all right?" she asked. "It doesn't look too good."

"I'm fine," I said. "You should see the other guy. His face looked much worse."

"I bet." Charlotte smiled.

I wished I knew what to say.

"So, why are you out here?" I asked.

"Once you left the restaurant, I really got to thinking. I used to come out here almost every night."

"Why's that?"

"I would lie, but it seems like you might be the only person on the island who'd believe me."

She looked to her right and toward the beach. I leaned against the pier's railing.

Charlotte continued, "On some nights, if I came out late enough, I could see her."

"Who?" I asked.

"My grandmother's grandmomma. I couldn't see much, just her walking along the beach with an umbrella and that big hat of hers. She looked just like the pictures my momma would show me." Charlotte paused to smile. "She was so young when she died. My great-grandpa, her only kid, was barely a year old."

I gripped the railing harder, and my fingernails dug into the veneered wood.

"What was her name?" I asked, although I knew the answer.

"Florence. But she went by Flo."

"Is your last name Gibson, Charlotte?"

"It is!" she said, chuckling. "How'd you know? Have you been stalking me?"

"Of course not," I said. "It was nice to see you."

I turned and walked back toward the resort, stomach turning. My rapid heartbeat increased the pain in my eye and leg as blood pulsed through the broken veins. How many lives did George's actions touch? How many families were either ended or forever changed because of what he did? All to sell some newspapers. What about the lives the Maimer affected?

I leaned over the railing and threw up. A few others on the pier reacted audibly in disgust.

Thankfully, Kurt was out of view of what had happened, although my breath could still give it away. I escaped the situation, steeped in embarrassment. I rounded a corner and found Kurt there, rocking in one of the chairs.

"Hey," I said through heavy breaths.

"Who was that?" Kurt asked, smirking.

"No one. Listen, I don't want to go out again tonight. Let's just go back to the room, okay? Maybe we'll try again tomorrow."

"Henry," Kurt said, his smile vanishing. "I can't stay, remember? I need to go home."

"You're staying, Kurt. I need you here."

"I'm sorry, but we talked about this. I have to go. My sister's graduation is tomorrow."

"Kurt," I said, trying to remain calm. "Don't make me say it again. You *owe* me."

"When are you going to let that go?" Kurt asked, standing up. "You should be thanking me. The podcast sure took off."

"I saved you from a lot of trouble on New Year's. But I can bring all that trouble back if you don't stay."

"It was an accident!" Kurt shouted.

Excerpt from The Cadaver Hour (originally recorded January 2, 2024)

"Very exciting day for the podcast, my loyal listeners. It seems the Maimer is back! That's right, he began 2024 with a brand-new victim. Maybe his New Year's resolution was to get back to doing things that bring him joy. And one of those things is killing. If that's the case, then it only took him a few hours.

"Twenty-three-year-old Brian Stevens's body was found dumped outside Marie College's planetarium on Monday. Perhaps the Maimer was avoiding the heavy security the college is now under. For those unaware, the planetarium is detached from the main campus and sits on a hill just a few blocks from what some are calling 'Murder Pond.' All the signatures of our local killer were present, proving this was his handiwork. Missing ears. Stab wounds. I wonder what Jim Upton is thinking. Is he realizing his fame is vanishing? He probably can't wait to leave this world now.

"I told you all, and I was right. The Maimer is still out there and very much a threat. Make sure you're home before dark, kids. I have no doubt this is the first in a string of victims that will soon emerge..."

"I CAN'T DO THE rest of this trip alone," I said. "Just give me this weekend, and I'll never bring it up again. Promise."

Kurt walked in a circle, then turned his back to me and stared out into the night. He sighed.

"Fine," he said. "Just one more day."

"Thank you."

I sat down and put my head in my hands. The smell of blood and sweat and fear from New Year's came rushing back. I don't think Kurt ever realized how scary that experience was for me. He was right, it was an accident. Kurt had had a few too many, and hadn't seen Brian crossing the street. When I got his frantic call, I made a decision. The Maimer would claim another victim. We were careful. No fingerprints. No drops of sweat fell on Brian's mangled body. And so far, we had gotten away with it. Better yet, we had benefited. The podcast's monthly listeners tripled.

I once asked Kurt why he had called my phone that night instead of one of his parents'. Maybe they could've covered it up. They had money, influence. But Kurt had said I was the first person he'd thought of. He felt like I was the only person in his life who would know what to do in that situation. And he was right.

We both got ready for bed after making our way back to the room. I tried to talk to Kurt, but he refused to give me more than one word for an answer.

Kurt turned out the lights and my eyes refused to close. It was easier to focus on the ceiling fan, so I noted each curve and spiral of the brass frame. Occasionally, I'd turn over and check the clock. Kurt's snoring was louder than the night before. Maybe I could do something good with this trip. Good for someone other than myself.

I thought of something. I chewed on the idea for almost the entire night. When I realized it was the right thing, my eyes felt heavy. The last time I remember seeing on the clock was four in the morning.

Excerpt from The Cadaver Hour (originally recorded February 16, 2024)

"…I hope everyone had a wonderful Valentine's Day. I know one person who did. Our local killer spent his night with one lucky, or unlucky, lady. But this time, the Maimer changed his demographic. Seventy-year-old homeless woman Regina Olsen was found dead just a few blocks from Marie College. Perhaps security was a little too tight and so he was forced to expand his hunting grounds? Maybe he just got bored of prowling the same area? Either way, we have a new victim. The woman's rough life was cut short on Wednesday. Might I say the Maimer did her a favor?

"The two lovebirds spent their final moments together in an embrace that left one of them covered in blood. The Maimer, poor guy, just loves a little too hard.

"But jokes aside, the Maimer is back and there's no question the police got the wrong guy. Everyone in Atlanta is in danger,

and you can be sure The Cadaver Hour *will cover each and every murder along the way...*"

Croquet Regulations

- No spiked shoes may be worn on croquet lawn.
- Wickets shall be placed on painted lines to prevent deterioration of playing surface.
- Please do not play music on speakers of any kind.
- No food or drink is allowed on croquet lawn.
- Games shall move along promptly.
- Please do not begin a new game if others are waiting to play.
- Mallets shall not be thrown, slammed, or otherwise violently depart the player's control.
- Croquet balls shall not become airborne.
- Any form of horseplay or other dangerous play is STRICTLY PROHIBITED.

Sunday, June 9, 2024

My head throbbed as I sat up in bed, the morning light burrowing into my skull.

It felt as if the one drink I had at the bar the night before was ten.

It felt as if my brain was stuffed with decay.

I felt as bad as Walter Alexander looked.

My right eye, now almost swollen shut, pained with the slightest touch. My leg felt better, but it was sensitive. A thin scab had formed, and I'd need to be careful so it could heal. It'd probably leave a nasty scar. I turned over, and the clock next to the bed read 11:00 a.m.

I sprang up. The last time I had slept that late was in college.

"Kurt?" I asked the empty room.

"Out here," Kurt called from the open balcony door.

Kurt sat overlooking the grounds, coffee resting on one of the chair's arms. He was reading from the book I had brought.

"I made a breakfast run," he said. "There's a sausage, egg, and cheese bagel on the table."

"Thanks."

"How's your eye? It looks worse."

"Not great," I said, grimacing. "I can barely see out of it."

"I'm sorry," he said. "Maybe you should get it checked out."

"It's fine."

"So, what's the plan today?" Kurt asked.

"Give me a minute to get myself together and we'll talk about it."

After eating the cold sandwich and making myself some coffee, I got ready for the day. The shower did more harm than good. Both hot and cold water stung my injuries. I got dressed and sat on the bed.

Kurt came back in. I could tell he was waiting for my direction.

"First thing I need to do is get my car taken care of. I'll be lucky if it's not already towed."

"I'll give you a ride out there, assuming you're okay with riding in my piece of junk." Kurt smiled.

"I am," I said. "After that, let's go over the videos and pictures from the last two nights."

"Why now? Can't that wait until we get back home?"

"I want to see George tonight," I said. "And I'm hoping something on those cameras can tell us where to find him."

I tried not to look at the dent on the front of Kurt's car as we approached. Once inside, after Kurt selected the perfect thrash metal CD to play, I looked around at his junk car. Pins held up the felt ceiling. A thin layer of grime coated the console in the middle. A mass of papers peeked through the cracked glove box.

"If you don't mind me asking," I said, elbow on the sticky arm rest. "Why don't you drive something a little more...of the last two decades?"

"I like this one," Kurt said, hands on ten and two. "But the real answer is this is all I can afford."

"I've been to your house. Your parents can afford a new car."

"My parents want to teach me the value of a dollar. They think if I grow up like a spoiled rich kid, I'll act like one. Apparently, Uncle Tim, my mom's brother, scared my parents into thinking that way."

"What happened to him?" I asked.

"I have no idea. My mom won't tell me. She just keeps saying, 'You don't want to end up like Uncle Tim.' My sister thinks he's in prison somewhere in Kansas."

"Interesting," I said.

My parents didn't have the choice to withhold wealth from me, but that was probably for the best. Uncle Tim and I might've been cellmates if I had grown up around the money Kurt had.

We found my car sitting where I'd left it, a bright orange parking ticket stuck under one of the windshield wipers. I crumpled up the ticket and tossed it into a nearby trash can.

About an hour later the tow truck came, and I paid the driver to haul it twenty miles to the nearest charger. It took another hour to get the car full of electricity.

I drove back to the resort and headed up to meet Kurt in the room. I walked in to find that Kurt, laptop open, had already begun reviewing the videos from both cameras.

"Did you find anything?" I asked.

He turned to me; his pensive face scrunched.

"What's wrong?"

"All these ghosts...*people* are saying George killed them. Is that true?"

"I think so," I said.

"Why would he do it? Some of them were kids."

"I don't know. That's why I want to confront him tonight."

"What's that going to do?" Kurt asked with a little more sharpness.

"If we can record him admitting to the crimes, it'll help us prove he was the Crane Island Killer. I know it's been a long time, but maybe some of the victims' families can get some closure."

Kurt relaxed. I could tell he liked the idea.

"But won't that hurt your family's reputation?"

"Probably," I said. "But our podcast audience doesn't even know who I really am."

Kurt stared at the ground, thinking it all over.

"How are you going to get a confession out of him?"

"I'll make up a confession of my own. Maybe ask for advice."

"A confession?" Kurt asked. "You don't mean New Year's—"

"No. Not that one."

"All right," Kurt said, nodding. "But first we need to find him."

I joined Kurt in front of his laptop and watched the videos back. They were all how I remembered them. My heart raced as the Alexander Cottage appeared on the screen and I was brought back to that horrifying encounter. Kurt had to look away when Walter's face appeared in stunning detail. I re-watched each recording again, going frame by frame to find something. Anything.

There was nothing.

I picked up Kurt's roommate's camera and scrolled back to the first recordings. There were two test videos, each only a few seconds long, Kurt had taken when we first arrived at Jones Cottage. I went all the way back to the first thing the camera captured: the photo Kurt accidentally took. It was the only frame where the flash was used. I brought the picture up on the laptop and scanned it.

There was a dark outline in the corner of the room, just behind me.

Kurt made some adjustments to the photo that made the figure more visible.

It looked as if two brothers were standing close to each other. It was easy to see why the ghosts kept mistaking me for him.

It was George Dean, staring at me and smiling.

We were going back to Jones Cottage.

Excerpt from The Cadaver Hour (originally recorded March 29, 2024)

"...A warm welcome to all our new listeners. As you may know, The Cadaver Hour *has now reclaimed the title of number one true crime podcast in the nation.*

"We can finally move on from talking about the Maimer's previous victim because we have two new ones to report on. The man and woman, I won't bother mentioning their names, were killed near where Regina Olsen tragically lost her life. This time, the killer left something behind. Our local monster stabbed the two victims with so much force the knife blade broke in half. It was sticking out of the male victim's back when investigators arrived at the scene. Police reports tell us the murder weapon was likely a chef's knife.

"I'm sure all our listeners have a similar knife at home. It's no surprise it broke during the attack. Those knives are much too thin to withstand the impact of dozens of punctures. Slicing a tomato? Sure. But cutting through clothes, skin, and cartilage?

The Maimer should know by now he needs to find something more suitable for his line of work..."

"My goodness, he *does* look like you," Kurt said.

I grunted an affirmation. It was difficult to see in the picture, but our matching jawline and nose were hard to miss.

"Hey, Henry?" Kurt said, closing his laptop. "I think I'm going to go for a swim before dinner. I've wanted to check out the pool since I got here. Is that all right?"

I smiled, "I think that'd be fine. But can you do me a favor first?"

"Of course. What is it?"

"Can you run down to the lobby and see if they have a first aid kit? I want to wrap up my leg."

"Will do," Kurt said as if I had put him in charge of something important. "Where are we going for dinner?"

"Wherever you want. Your pick. I'll get you whatever meal you're hungry for."

"I'll figure that out while sunbathing."

Kurt left and came back with a small first aid kit, then left the room again after changing into his swimsuit.

I spent the next few hours trying to distract myself from what I'd be doing later that night. After washing my leg, I wrapped it in gauze from the kit and tried to stay off it as much as possible. I lay in bed, then moved to the balcony.

Kurt returned around six, cheeks red from the sun.

"How was it?" I asked.

"Great," he said. "Lots of kids having fun, splashing around."

I remembered the kids being annoying, but I was glad Kurt enjoyed it.

"Did you decide where you'd like to eat?" I asked.

"Yes," he said. "I want to eat at the resort's restaurant. The internet says they've got amazing fried chicken."

"Good choice," I said, smiling.

After getting ready, we headed downstairs for dinner. I passed the same art, pictures, and ornate furniture I had when I first arrived. The hotel's decor, once charming, now felt phony. I noticed the cracks and dust I had been blind to. The intricate designs of the chair's gaudy fabrics seemed forced and excessive. The warmth they once held was gone.

Our meal was eaten mostly in silence. I wasn't sure why Kurt was so quiet, but I was busy thinking about Jones Cottage. I didn't know what I'd say to George, or if he'd even show up. If we were to expose him, would he try to murder us just like the rest of his victims? The Alexanders had gotten close to killing me, but if anyone could finish the job, it'd be him. I reminded myself I was doing something good. It was worth the risk.

Kurt seemed to enjoy his food, which might as well have been from the kids' menu. For my meal, which could've been my last, I ordered a filet mignon with all the fixings. I also got the most expensive pour of whiskey they had. It didn't taste much different from the stuff I had at home, but I was glad to have tried it. I don't think I quite appreciated all the flavors.

Once finished, another generous cash tip given, we got up and returned to the room to prepare and wait for sundown.

To pass the time, and to distract us, we put on another movie. Another comedy.

Unfortunately, there was a touching scene toward the end about a dog and I thought of Rambo. I hoped he was doing all right at the daycare. Who would take care of him if something happened to me later that night?

Like on Saturday, the room was dark when the movie finished. Kurt and I sat in silence as the credits rolled, unable to face what was next. It wasn't until the next movie played for ten minutes that I forced my body out of paralysis. I considered not going at all, but I wasn't sure if I could convince Kurt to stay another night. I had already pushed him hard enough.

Finally, I stood up and Kurt followed.

Kurt and I got ready, taking much longer than necessary. I grabbed the big camera, the walkie-talkies, and the two lapel mics. I triple-checked each one. As I picked up my phone from the dresser, the crystals caught my eye. I shoved them in my left pocket.

"Aren't you going to put on the protective gear?" Kurt asked.

"No," I said. "I think that would make him suspicious. Plus, I trust that you'll come in when I need you."

Kurt nodded and we exited the room.

"So, how are we going to do this?" Kurt asked as we walked down the hall.

"I'll go in alone," I said. "I'll do my best to get a confession. You wait outside and come in when I tell you."

"What if I hear a scream?" Kurt asked.

"I think that's a safe bet to come inside. I need you to be ready. We're dealing with a very dangerous ghost here."

"Poltergeist," Kurt said.

"What?"

"The spirits on the island would be considered poltergeists. Ghosts can't interact with the real world, but these can."

"Right," I said, shaking my head. "Just make sure you come in when I say so, phone up and recording a video. If we can get George to disappear on camera, that'd be even better."

The Jones Cottage was a short walk away. About halfway to the cottage, I turned around and faced the resort. I thought about running back, but the resort's unwelcoming silence deterred me. On Friday, it seemed to inhale the ocean waves and exhale jazz music and excited voices. That Sunday, it was quiet. It was as if, in the time between the weekend and Monday morning, it wasn't meant to be seen. It reminded me of Crane Island's ghosts, witnessing a world they were never meant to.

"You coming?" Kurt asked.

"Yeah," I said, turning back again.

Our voices and footsteps stood out against the still night, the waves the only sound helping to mask them. I found myself looking over my shoulder more than the last two ghost hunts. Every sound made me flinch. Kurt sneezed and my hands moved to cover my chest.

When we arrived at the Jones Cottage, it hummed with energy. The frequency matched the vibration in my bones. The force was stronger than any I had felt before. I knew George was inside.

Kurt and I tested the walkie-talkies, and I told him to stay far enough away so as to not interfere, but close enough to hear a scream.

"Good luck," Kurt whispered.

I took a deep breath, started recording on the big camera, and entered the cottage.

The thick air inside almost needed to be chewed before being breathed in. I flicked on a flashlight and scanned the room. The corner where Rose Jones and her father were Friday night was empty, at least for now.

My ears popped. I closed my eyes and raised my arms over my head to protect myself. When I straightened back up, I felt something behind me. It was as if my head was a radio turned to a static channel. As I turned, the connection became clearer, and the noise lessened. I didn't bring the flashlight up right away, but I didn't need it to know I was face to face with George Dean.

At the same instant, I flipped both the camera and the light up.

It was him, smiling at me the same way I smiled for pictures.

I was too stunned to speak. I knew I should take charge of the conversation so we'd get where I wanted to go, but I couldn't find the words. His dark suit and gloves made it difficult to see what the rest of his body was doing. It was as if I was looking at myself in a different time.

"Look at you," George said. "It's like looking in a mirror."

"H...Hello," I said.

"Who are you?" he said.

"I'm Henry...Henry Hall. We're related."

His eyes lit up and he took a step toward me. I moved back with a matching step.

"I knew there was something special about you," he said, his voice even sounding like mine. "Ever since you came here a couple nights ago. Normally all I can do is ruffle a newspaper or spill some coffee. I've never been able to appear like this. You make me feel so powerful. I wonder if I can..."

George reached for the nearest wall and his hand stopped when it pressed against the crumbling paint. He looked back at me and smiled, genuine this time. He kicked a nearby chair and was delighted when it toppled over. The noise echoed off the walls.

"Remarkable," he said. "Here I am with my own flesh and blood. However, I did think you'd dress a little better."

I looked down. My jeans and T-shirt probably appeared to him as something a poor farmer would wear. If I was going to get anything out of George, I needed him to like me.

"I'm actually...pretty famous," I said.

"Is that right? Has our family become prominent once again?"

"Well...no. People...hundreds of thousands of people know me by my podcast name."

"Podcast?" he asked. "What's that?"

"It's like a radio show," I said.

"What about power?" George asked. "Influence? Have you met the president?"

"I haven't."

"Embarrassing," he said, turning away from me. "You didn't do a thing with what I built."

I felt defensive.

"What you built?" I asked. "You left us with nothing."

"That wasn't my fault!" he yelled.

Was that how I sounded when I raised my voice at the bartender? George adjusted his suit jacket and let a long breath out.

"Please forgive me," George said. "That wound is still fresh."

It was time to steer the conversation toward what I came here for. People, no matter what time period, love to give advice.

"Listen, George, my radio show isn't as popular as it could be. Do you know how I could get more listeners? I'm willing to do anything. Our family has been struggling since you died."

He began pacing back and forth and I followed his every step with the camera and flashlight.

"I may be able to help you," he said. "I'll let you in on a little secret. I want our family to thrive once again. But first you must turn that camera off."

"Of course," I said, setting the camera on the floor, but not stopping recording. I made sure it was still pointed in his direction. "It's off."

"Good. I'll start by asking you something. How far would you go for success?"

"Far," I said.

"Would you...kill for your radio show?"

It was time for a confession of my own. One that would hopefully open George up to talk about his crimes.

"Yes," I said without delay. "I have already."

George smiled, "Then we are one and the same, my boy. Nothing sells more papers or attracts more attention than murder. Sometimes you must be willing to get your hands dirty."

"Did you kill the Alexanders?" I asked. "Or the Jones family?"

"All unfortunate casualties of my rise to the top. Each of my victims sliced and dumped into the ocean. Tell me, Henry, did you savor your victims' last breaths before you took their life?"

"I did," I said. "And after, I'd dump them in the pond for the fish to nibble on."

"Incredible! We disposed of our bodies the same way. Do they have a name for you?"

"The Marie College Maimer."

"College students?" George asked. "How tragic."

"What did they call you?"

"Have you heard of the Crane Island Killer?" George asked.

"I have," I said. "Was that you?"

"In the flesh," he said, taking a bow.

He confirmed what I had suspected since my first night on the island. I'd wanted to believe, however unlikely, it wasn't true. Our family's lost fortune was built on murder. Even worse, the murder of children and entire families.

"Do people still know the name?" George asked.

"They do," I said.

"They never found out it was me, did they?"

"No."

I had the recorded confession. It was time to get out of there.

"Thank you for your wisdom, George. I'm going to put it to use—"

"You don't think I'm that much of a dolt, do you?" he asked, his voice turning sharp.

"What?" I asked.

He walked forward and stomped on the camera, shattering it.

"You were trying to catch me, weren't you, Henry?"

"No, I was—"

"You think you're going to be the big man who solved the Crane Island Killer mystery, don't you?"

"George, I—"

"Well, now it's only me and you, my boy," he said, standing close.

He put a gloved hand on my shoulder. Even though we were the same height, he felt much taller. Was that the same hand he used to kill?

"You wouldn't want to spoil my reputation, would you?" he asked.

His breath smelled of coffee and cigar smoke. The boiling anger returned to my stomach. We should've been rich. I remembered all the bullying. All the teasing and crying and anger. All the venomous words my dad had spit at my mom. I twisted out of his grasp and took a few steps back.

"There's nothing to spoil," I said. "I grew up like everyone else. What happened to all the money? The *power*? *Influence*?"

"It was taken from me," George said. "My last piece of advice, Henry, is if you kill for your success, make sure they're dead."

"Eileen?" I asked.

"Yes," he said. "My hand was forced. I sold the newspaper. I emptied my savings and liquidated my bonds until bankruptcy. All to raise the money I needed to keep her and police quiet. I was ruined!"

Kurt's family's money was *my* money. The Greene's house should've been the one I grew up in.

The rage boiled over.

"I'm telling everyone!" I shouted. "You're a failure!"

"Now, Henry," George said.

"You could've worked harder and built the wealth back up. But you had to die of a heart attack. Was that a lie, too?"

"Pardon me?" he said, bringing a hand to his chest.

"You had a heart attack and died," I said as if stating the obvious. "You left your kids with nothing."

"That's news to me. Last thing I remember I was out on the balcony, trying to forget the whole mess. My butler handed me a coffee that was some new blend."

The butler's words returned to me.

I'm pleased to see you harbor no ill will toward me after what happened. You must know, I did it to protect the both of us.

"You were killed by your own butler," I said, laughing. "He didn't trust you to keep your big mouth shut. You're nothing."

"Quiet," George said, reaching behind his back and producing a foot-long hunting knife. "You're the liar."

He walked toward me, blade reflecting my flashlight's beam.

"Kurt," I said into my walkie-talkie. "Come inside. Now!"

George raised the knife above his head.

Kurt stumbled inside the cottage behind me. I turned to look at him, thankful he had saved me. His phone was up with the flash on.

"Henry," Kurt said, his eyes fixed on something just over my shoulder.

"What?" I turned back.

George didn't disappear. He stood there, hand behind his back.

"And who's this?" George asked.

"I'm...Kurt...sir."

Kurt's voice gave away his fear. I hoped George couldn't hear it, too.

"Another relative?" George asked. "Because I feel a strong connection to you as well."

"No," Kurt said. "My last name is Greene."

"Greene?" George asked. "The same Greene as...Eileen Greene?"

"Yes," Kurt said. "Did you know her? She was my relative."

George's face turned down in horror, then morphed into a nasty snarl. Even after one hundred years, his hate didn't fade.

George revealed the knife and ran at Kurt.

In an instant, I reacted. I tackled George and felt something sharp bite into my bicep as we hit the floor. George shoved me off him and I stood, staring at the knife sticking out of my arm. It wasn't a deep cut, so the knife fell and banged against the wood floor. I grabbed my arm as the pain surged through my body. Blood seeped through my fingers.

George reached for the knife, but before his fingers closed around it, Kurt grabbed it and sank it into his back.

Seeing George on the ground, his own blade sticking out of his back, made him look much less powerful than the image I had of him for so many years.

Kurt looked to me, his expression both shocked at what he had just done and proud at the revenge he had carried out for Eileen.

But George didn't disappear.

He began laughing. He reached behind him and pulled the knife out.

"You can't hurt a ghost," he said. "I'm already dead."

There was nothing more I could do. My legs refused to move. I thought we should both run, but I had no time to react, and I couldn't leave Kurt here alone with him.

I felt my pockets with my good arm.

The crystals. They were warm as if activated by their proximity to a hateful spirit.

They were my last resort. I hoped the lady Kurt bought them from knew what she was talking about.

George took a step toward us and as he did, I pulled the crystals out and held them up.

He groaned and dropped the knife.

I brought them closer, his yells becoming more and more agonizing.

"Stop," he groaned.

I almost did. He had tried to kill us, but he was still someone I was related to. He was still an immense success who achieved what I could only dream of. But he was also a killer. One who preyed on innocent people who didn't deserve their end. A monster.

I touched them to George's body, but he didn't disappear.

If we couldn't kill a ghost, then what could?

"Henry!" Kurt shouted. "It's her!"

Eileen's ghost stepped out from the shadows. Her maid's outfit bounced with every step. I could see the resemblance to Kurt clearer when she wasn't wet and covered in blood.

Eileen picked up the knife and walked over to where George was shouting, weak from the crystals.

"No!" George yelled. "You can't!"

Eileen plunged the knife into George's chest. After a last distressed cry, they both were gone.

My vision became dizzy, and I fell to my knees.

"Henry!" Kurt said, rushing to my side. "Are you okay?"

"I need to go to a hospital," I said.

"I'll take you."

My arm was losing blood fast.

Kurt helped me all the way to his car and found the nearest hospital on his phone.

As I sat in the passenger seat, being as careful as possible to not spill any blood on the seats, I thought about what George had told me. It was so easy for people to do horrible things to each other, just for some money that meant nothing in the end. For as long as I bore it, I'd hate my middle name.

I looked at Kurt, who was driving as fast as he could. If there was anyone I'd want to have my family's money, it was him. I wouldn't even be alive if it wasn't for the crystals he'd bought. The Dean wealth was in good hands. His parents had nothing to worry about when it came to raising a spoiled kid. They should buy him a new car as soon as possible. If they didn't, I would.

NELSON'S

BAR & LOUNGE

1880s

Morning Glory

Cogncac - Whiskey - Simple Syrup - Curacao - Bitters

1900s

The Last Word

Gin - Green Chartreuse - Maraschino - Lime

Caipirinha

Cachaca - Lime - Demerara Sugar

1920s

Prohibition Daiquiri

Imported Rum - Lime - Simple Syrup

Bees Knees

Imported Gin - Honey - Lemon

1940s

El Diablo

Tequila - Creme de Cassis - Lime - Ginger Beer

Screwdriver

Vodka - Orange - Orange Bitters

Monday, June 10, 2024

My own bed's soft sheets and the train's horn welcomed me as I woke up. The stitches in my right arm throbbed after I wiped the sleep from my eyes.

I stumbled out of bed, got ready for the day, and treated myself to an expensive breakfast. I savored every bite, knowing this was the last time I'd have the meal of my choice. After a night's sleep, I was even more confident in what I wanted to do that day. I would do what George was never strong enough to. I opened my closet, grabbed a bag of items, and threw them into my car before driving to the podcast studio.

Kurt's absence was apparent. I had a tough time setting up the equipment, but he deserved the day off. He had stayed by my side throughout the entire hospital visit and drove us both back to Atlanta in the middle of the night.

When I saw what happened to George, it felt as if I was looking at my future. Not just my appearance, but my fate. All the ghosts I had met on Crane Island had their lives destroyed by my relative. The Maimer had done the same. What was it all for? Some money that vanished before George died? Even if he hadn't lost it all, it would've been meaningless after George's last breath.

There was always going to be an Eileen. Mine just hadn't happened yet.

Once everything was ready and recording, I began.

Excerpt from The Cadaver Hour (recorded June 10, 2024)

"Hello, listeners. This is, of course, your favorite podcast host Hank Blight. But it's time I reveal my real name. I am Henry Dean Hall, great-great-great-grandson of George Dean. This is the last episode I will be recording. It will be less of a show and more of a confession.

My trip to the Georgia barrier island was very successful. Not only did I capture video that proves ghosts exist, but I solved a cold case that was over one hundred years old. If you check out our website in a day or two, you will see that my beloved co-host and sound engineer, Kurt Greene, has uploaded footage that proves George Dean, the once-famous newspaperman, was the Crane Island Killer. But why did George Dean do it? To sell more newspapers, of course.

"As I've said many times, I'm dedicated to the truth. I almost lost an arm trying to solve the case! If it wasn't for Kurt, I might not be here right now. George was not happy when I got him to con-

fess. He smashed my expensive camera. But guess what, George? It wasn't a film camera. The memory card was salvaged, and it contained the entire thing. He hadn't even noticed my lapel mic or its red light.

"But that's not the only case I'll be solving on today's episode. There is a similar set of murders that have been perpetrated for the same reasons as the Crane Island killings. As I'm sure you all know, the Marie College Maimer has been terrorizing the Atlanta area for over six months now. Well, if you watch the video, you'll hear I admitted to being the Maimer. At first, I did this to pull a confession out of George Dean. But I'm here to tell you it was the truth. I am the Maimer. Or, I should say, I'm the second Maimer. I killed Brian Stevens. I killed Regina Olsen and the two victims after her. I took up the mantle of the Maimer when Jim Upton was caught. The police got the right man. But after that, I saw an opportunity and took it. Why did I do it? To keep you all listening.

"Once I hit publish on this show, I'll wait for the police to arrive at the studio. They will find the broken knife as well as Connor Inman's wallet.

"It's also important that I admit that the exclusive information I've been sharing about the Maimer victims has all been lies. Lies to keep you tuning in.

"Which one of you will be the first to call the police? I suspect it'll be one of my most loyal fans.

"It's time to let the ghosts sleep. Both at Marie College and on Crane Island.

"Thank you for all your support over the last few years. I will be leaving the podcast to my best friend, Kurt Greene."

An immense weight lifted from my shoulders. This way, unlike George, I was going out on my own terms. I stopped the recording and sat back in the chair. Kurt wouldn't have time to get any ideas from the butler.

I clicked the publish button and waited.

Our History

Crane Island Resort opened in 1879 thanks to the vision of Nelson Tybee, who saw the potential for a coastal getaway for Atlanta elites. As the word spread, guests came from farther and farther away to enjoy our Georgia hospitality. Not even a local murder spree in the early 1900s could staunch the flow of visitors!

The 1920s brought a new challenge in the form of prohibition. Nelson's Bar was forced to find new suppliers—rum runners! Soon after, Crane Island became a favorite of gangsters and mafiosos in search of a southern escape.

Today, guests still travel from far and wide to visit the historic Crane Island resort and experience our luxurious brand of Georgia hospitality in a beachfront setting.

Epilogue

Excerpt from The Cadaver Hour (recorded December 6, 2024)

"Hi everyone, Kurt here, welcoming you back to the most-listened-to true crime podcast in the nation. Thank you for all the support you've given me since I've taken over. It means so much.

"After a lot of convincing, my parents finally let me make a trip down to see Henry at Valdosta State Prison. He wanted to thank all the loyal listeners who have sent him mail over the last few months. He even said some of the inmates were fans of The Cadaver Hour. *Henry is doing well, but he misses his dog. I assured him Rambo is doing just fine with us. He loves having a big backyard. It looks like Henry will get the death penalty, but he's hoping it'll be a while before...you know.*

"A few streaming services are already working on a documentary about the whole thing. We've had enormous offers to buy the rights to the footage we captured on Crane Island. Henry thinks

I should take the money and donate it to a variety of charities, especially those supporting the Marie College victims.

"Anyway, onto the show. First, I'd like to bring back one of my favorite segments: local crimes. A murder took place over the weekend with some very familiar elements..."

Acknowledgements

I owe a great debt of thanks to my writing critique group: Daniel Cozart, Allan Dodson, Taylor Davidson, Michael Austin, Greg Juhn, Matthew Evans, and Chris Narvaez. Their ideas and edits are all over this story. Without their help, this book would barely be readable. I hope their future beach trips go better than Henry's.

For their support of indie authors and their love for the horror genre, I'm grateful to everyone at Undertaker Books. Thank you to D.L. Winchester, Rebecca Cuthbert, and Cyan LeBlanc for their assistance and hard work during the publishing process.

Thank you to Jekyll Island and the Jekyll Island Club Resort for providing the inspiration for many of the locations in this story.

And finally, my wonderful family. I am deeply grateful to my parents, Scott and Elizabeth Agre, for their belief in me. With love and thanks to my partner, Caitlin Franchini, for her encouragement when I needed it most. Special thanks to our beagle, Banjo, whose many walks allowed me time to think about this story and plan what would come next.

About Keller Agre

Keller Agre is a new horror fiction writer originally from Overland Park, Kansas whose work has appeared in various publications including Undertaker Books and Haunted Words Press. He writes both short stories as well as longer pieces. *Let the Ghosts Sleep* is his first novella. He is a member of the Atlanta Writers Club as well as various book clubs in the Atlanta area. You can usually find him hiking the Appalachian Mountains, playing folk music on his guitar, or walking his beagle, Banjo. He works as a Treasury Analyst and lives in Decatur, Georgia with his partner, Caitlin.

UB Website

If you are a fan of horror stories and tales,
you'll want to follow Undertaker Books.
We're bringing you stories to take to your grave.

Made in the USA
Columbia, SC
15 June 2025

59231621R00091